RETURNING TO LOVE

STARLIGHT RIDGE
BOOK 6

KAT BELLEMORE

KB PRESS

ABOUT THIS BOOK

Love is a young person's game.
Or so she'd been told.

Thirty years. That's how long it has been since Jessie Carter and her ex-fiance, Erwin, had a fight so massive that it fueled town gossip for weeks.

Thirty years since she'd given him his ring back.

Thirty years that they've had to continue seeing each other, because neither of them managed to leave their small town.

Thirty years of Jessie playing matchmaker for everyone but herself.

And it's been one week since Erwin showed up on her doorstep, flowers in hand.

It's too little, too late, by her estimation.

But Erwin is nearing his sixtieth birthday, and all he wants is one chance. One chance to stop their thirty-year feud. Once chance to no longer be alone.

And Jessie is tempted to give it to him.

ALSO BY KAT BELLEMORE

BORROWING AMOR

Borrowing Amor

Borrowing Love

Borrowing a Fiancé

Borrowing a Billionaire

Borrowing Kisses

Borrowing Second Chances

STARLIGHT RIDGE

Diving into Love

Resisting Love

Starlight Love

Building on Love

Winning his Love

Returning to Love

1

Jessie walked quickly from her home, a basket filled with her world-famous tarts hanging from one arm. They were famous here in the small town of Starlight Ridge, anyway. The scent of lemon escaped from under the towel that covered them, and she had to fight the temptation to sneak a couple. You'd think after thirty years of baking tarts for every town event, every new arrival, and every bake sale that she'd be sick of them. If anything, her love for them had only grown.

"Jessie, where are you headed to in such a hurry?" Grant Mueller called from the doorway of Mueller Market, the only place to purchase groceries in town. He and his wife had owned it as long as Jessie could remember. That was the nice thing about a place like Starlight Ridge. Everyone knew each other, and everyone cared. There weren't many who moved away, and even fewer who chose to move in.

Today was an exception, though.

"Off to deliver my welcome basket for the young woman who just arrived," Jessie said, lifting her basket into the air, as if she needed to prove it.

Grant glanced up the road, looking guilty. "Been meaning to get on that. We'll probably head over tomorrow with some fresh produce. Possibly the next day. Do you think that's too late?"

As head of the welcoming committee, Jessie always encouraged the town to visit newcomers within two days of their arrival. Any longer than that and she felt it started getting awkward. But if it was just the Muellers, she supposed it would help spread out the visits a little.

"I'm sure she will appreciate the visit, no matter when she gets it," Jessie said with a smile, and then continued her walk up the road until she reached a small bungalow. It used to belong to Isaac, a resident surfer-slash-lifeguard. Until he'd gone and married Leanne, his childhood sweetheart. They now lived in, and ran, her family's bed and breakfast.

There had been a couple of rocky years when Isaac and Leanne's relationship had seemed doomed to fail— one of them running off to Hollywood could do that—and Jessie credited herself for being the catalyst that had helped them finally work things out and walk down the aisle. Her success hadn't been surprising, considering she was responsible for many of the romantic matches in town.

It was a gift, and one Jessie was more than willing to bestow upon Starlight Ridge. She figured that even if she wasn't meant for a happily-ever-after, at least she could help others find theirs.

When Jessie knocked on the bungalow's door, she half-expected Isaac to answer in his board shorts, wearing an easy smile. Instead, she was met with a woman who was quite a bit older than Jessie had been expecting. The woman was probably in her late fifties or early sixties—around Jessie's age. So, not *old*. But also not the young woman Jessie had expected to meet.

Jessie's surprise must have been obvious because the woman gave an uncertain smile, like she was anticipating trouble. "Can I help you?"

Jessie straightened and stuck out a hand. "Jessie Carter. I live down the road, and I would like to formally welcome you to Starlight Ridge."

"Thank you." The woman smiled and took Jessie's hand in hers. "My name is Barbara, but everyone calls me Barb."

That was a lovely name, and if Jessie was being honest, she was a little jealous that her own mother hadn't thought of it. But there was something a little off about Barbara. After a brief moment's consideration, Jessie determined that it was her smile. It seemed forced—almost as if she wasn't thrilled to see Jessie.

But that was ridiculous, so Jessie brushed it off as Barbara being nervous about moving to a new town. It was difficult, not knowing what to expect. Which was where the welcoming committee came in.

"It's lovely to meet you." Jessie held out the basket of tarts. "This is just the first of many welcome baskets you can expect to receive over the next couple of days. I know relocating can be overwhelming, but when you move to Starlight Ridge, you gain more than just new neighbors. You can consider us family."

Barbara took the basket from Jessie and lifted the towel. "Oh, these smell amazing. Did you bake them yourself?"

Jessie tried not to look overly proud when she said, "Why yes, I did. Not to brag, but these tarts are quite well known in these parts."

"Well, they look absolutely divine." Barbara replaced the towel. "I should probably set them in the fridge with Erwin's shrimp. They do need to be refrigerated, don't they?"

"Erwin's shrimp?" Jessie said, dumbfounded that she hadn't been the first to deliver her basket. She was always first.

"Oh, I know that the shrimp needs to be kept cold. I meant the tarts." A pause. "Erwin is his name, isn't it? The owner of the restaurant, Seaside Bay? He stopped by about half an hour ago."

The nerve of that man. He knew that as head of the

welcoming committee, Jessie was always first to welcome new residents. His cloak and dagger antics had worsened over the years, and Jessie didn't know what to do with him anymore. She'd tried the civil approach, but he'd only shrugged and carried on, like he couldn't care less.

There had been one point, many years earlier, when he had cared. A great deal.

But those times were over, and the man had become nothing but a thorn in Jessie's side.

"Jessie?" Barbara asked tentatively, like it hadn't been the first time she'd said her name.

Jessie shook herself from her thoughts. "Yes, his name is Erwin. And no, the tarts don't need to be refrigerated. In fact, they prefer room temperature. Just make sure to eat them in the next couple of days, and they'll be fine."

"Wonderful." Barbara gave a polite smile, and then silence fell over them.

Jessie had hoped Barbara would carry the conversation —she didn't want to be perceived as nosy—but when the quiet had gone on long enough to be awkward, Jessie asked, "What brought you here to Starlight Ridge?" She'd asked around, and no one seemed to know anything about the mysterious stranger. They'd even gotten her age wrong by a few decades.

Barbara hesitated, like she wasn't used to such personal questions from complete strangers. She'd have to get used to that. "I finally retired, and I knew I needed to go somewhere new. After my husband passed away last year, well, I couldn't escape fast enough. I needed somewhere quiet. Somewhere I could hear myself think."

Jessie understood that feeling well. Yes, she and Barbara were going to be good friends, indeed.

"You came to the right place," Jessie said. "Starlight Ridge is exactly what you need. Aside from tourist season. But as long as you stay away from the boardwalk during the summer months, you should be fine. Why don't you come to my place for dinner tonight, and then we can meander over to the sunset stroll and I can show you around? The sunsets here aren't to be missed, and the whole town gathers together each night, just to catch one of God's little miracles. I can save you a permanent spot next to me, if you want. I've always spent the evenings alone, and it would be nice to have someone to talk to."

Had that come across as needy? It probably had. But Jessie was so excited to have someone her own age move in —and who was single, no less—that it was difficult to harness it.

Barbara was still smiling, but it was strained. Jessie hadn't been imagining it, after all. "I'm sorry, but Erwin already invited me. For both dinner and the sunset stroll. Next time, though."

"Erwin?" Jessie stared, dumbfounded. The man didn't go out of his way to make friends, and she doubted he had gone on a date in decades. Probably since they—

Well, never mind that.

Jessie supposed there weren't a lot of options in

Starlight Ridge for people like them. People who were older and single. Good for Erwin. It would do him some good. Maybe even take his crankiness down a few notches.

"Is there anything about him I should know?" Barbara asked. "Tips or tricks? I'm so nervous—I haven't been on a date with someone other than my late husband in forty years. We were high school sweethearts." Her expression turned anxious. "You know, come to think of it, I've probably only been on a date with one or two other people in my lifetime. I don't know why I said yes. He caught me off guard. New town. New people. New experiences."

Barbara stepped back from the door, looking like she might hyperventilate, and Jessie rushed forward, resting a hand on Barbara's arm. Jessie's gaze landed on several other baskets sitting on the counter. Erwin hadn't been the only one to beat Jessie to welcoming Barbara.

She was losing her touch.

"You shouldn't feel pressured into something you're not ready for," Jessie said, turning her attention back to Barbara. "He'd understand."

"Would he, though?" Barbara asked. "I have no idea because I don't know anything about this place. Or this man. I've been in town less than six hours, and there's been an endless barrage of people and baskets and invitations. I wanted quiet. I wanted to be alone. And this is not it."

When Barbara's gaze landed somewhere beyond Jessie,

she glanced over her shoulder. Adeline was coming up the road, basket in hand.

"If it helps, Addie is bringing you the best chocolate truffles you'll ever eat," Jessie said, her voice weak.

She'd never had anyone tell her that the town's gifts weren't wanted—that their welcome wasn't needed. The town wasn't intruding—they were being inclusive. Making the newcomer feel at home.

Weren't they?

"I don't even have a phone number for Erwin," Barbara said, her voice rising in pitch. "He said he'd pick me up here at six-thirty."

Oh, that was a problem.

"He doesn't have a cell phone," Jessie said with an apologetic smile. "Doesn't believe in them. But you could call the restaurant."

That didn't help Barbara's anxiety. If anything, she now looked like she was going to throw up.

"Or I can stop by his place and deliver the news for you," Jessie hurriedly added. "No problem. I'll just tell him that you're a bit overwhelmed with so much change and to try again in a week or two."

Barbara held up a hand while shaking her head. She seemed to have calmed a bit, and her lips were pressed in a tight line. "No. I'll call and tell him myself. But I'm not rescheduling. Not in a week. Or two. Or three. I'm sure this is a lovely place, but it's not for me. Maybe when my husband and I were young and starting a family—it could have been nice. But I need quiet. Disconnect. A place to just...be. This isn't that place."

Jessie blinked rapidly, attempting to understand what was happening here. Barbara wouldn't really leave after arriving just that morning, would she?

"We can give you space," Jessie insisted, attempting some damage control. "This hill is the quietest one in town. You'll get a fantastic view of the ocean each morning, and the bungalow was meant for only one or two people, so you'll never feel obligated to invite guests over."

Barbara released a long breath and gave Jessie a kind smile, but Jessie already understood its meaning before the woman spoke. "You all seem like lovely people, but if this hill is the quietest in town, I'm going to have a problem."

Adeline appeared in the open doorway, as if proving her point.

"Knock knock," Adeline said. Her gaze landed on Jessie, and her eyes crinkled in amusement. "I wanted to welcome you to Starlight Ridge, but it looks like you've already met our fearless leader." She extended her basket toward Barbara. "I'm Adeline."

"Thank you. This is lovely," Barbara said, taking on the air of a gracious host as she accepted the chocolates.

"And there's plenty more welcome gifts coming your way," Adeline added. Jessie wished she wouldn't have. "In fact, I can guarantee you'll receive another three within the next twenty minutes. You won't have to shop for food for another week."

And that was the final nail in the coffin.

Barbara was struggling to keep her smile. "How kind," she squeaked out.

Jessie left the bungalow, knowing she'd never see Barbara again. It turned out that they weren't meant to be the best of friends—or even casual acquaintances.

Because by the following morning, when the next wave of welcome baskets had made their way to the bungalow, Barbara was already gone.

No one had seen a moving truck or a vehicle of any kind. But she, and all her belongings, had disappeared.

2

E rwin Peterson was a lot of things. Saxophone player. Restaurant owner. Old enough to receive a senior citizen discount.

But he hadn't realized that *naive* had been on that list. Or *self-deceiving*.

He hadn't thought he'd been imagining things when the new woman in town, Barbara, had smiled at him the way she had. It had been a long time since anyone had looked at him like that.

Too long.

About thirty years, give or take.

And she had agreed to go out to dinner with him.

Miracle of miracles.

Barbara had called Erwin at the restaurant only a couple of hours before he was due to pick her up for their date. At first he'd thought she was canceling. There had been a hesitancy in her voice, and she'd struggled finding the right words. Thankfully, he'd been able to read between the lines when she'd admitted that she hadn't been on a date with anyone but her late husband since high school.

Erwin had assured her that he was nervous too, and that this was a no-pressure date. Just two people getting something to eat and taking in the sites. The smoke alarm had then gone off in the restaurant's kitchen, and he'd had to give a hurried goodbye and hang up, glad they had gotten things cleared up.

He was now convinced that the smoke alarm had been an omen for what was to come.

Maybe he hadn't said the right things when they were at dinner. Maybe he'd talked too much about himself and hadn't asked enough questions about her.

Or maybe he hadn't talked enough.

Erwin wasn't exactly known for his conversational skills.

Whatever it had been, when they'd finished eating, Barbara had asked if she could skip the sunset stroll that evening and turn in early.

He supposed they were getting on in years and early evenings weren't uncommon among their demographic.

But then he'd learned during his morning walk that Barbara had left Starlight Ridge. Hadn't lasted twenty-four hours before she'd disappeared. And judging by the FOR

SALE sign in front of the bungalow, she wasn't coming back.

Had their date gone so badly that Barbara had felt the need to disappear and never return?

He knew it was ridiculous to think he wielded that much power. But even now, he couldn't help but wonder if he had scared her off. Asking a woman out to dinner— particularly a newcomer—wasn't Erwin's style. Maybe waiting a few days would have been proper etiquette.

Erwin didn't know much about etiquette.

As he turned a corner, his dog Donna leading the way, his gaze landed on a figure in the distance. Erwin came to an abrupt stop, causing the dog leash to become suddenly taut, and Donna stumbled backwards. She howled in protest, turning an accusing eye on Erwin.

"Sorry girl," he said, scratching her behind the ear. "But maybe we should go a different route today. Maybe skip the beach and walk up by the new library. Wouldn't that be fun? Try something new?"

Erwin was a creature of habit, as was Donna. but that included avoiding Jessie whenever possible. That was one habit that trumped all others.

Unfortunately, Jessie hadn't acquired the same taste for avoidance, and Erwin knew the moment she'd spotted him.

"Erwin," she called out, hurrying down the boardwalk toward him. "Erwin, what did you do?"

He turned as if he hadn't heard her, wondering if he

was too old to take up jogging. He already knew his knees would protest, and Jessie could easily outpace him, but a guy had to try.

"Erwin Peterson, I know you can hear me. You aren't so old that you've gone deaf. What did you do to Barbara?"

Of course Jessie would know about his and Barbara's date. She knew everything about everyone, sometimes even before those involved.

"Nothing," he grumbled, glancing back toward Jessie. "I didn't do a thing."

Despite the fact that moments earlier he'd been convinced he must have been the cause of Barbara leaving town so suddenly, he was now equally sure that it couldn't have been him. Erwin was nothing but an old man who should be preparing for retirement but instead managed a restaurant that only made a profit during tourist season.

Not exactly appealing to the ladies, but hardly threatening. Nothing that a *no, thank you* wouldn't have taken care of.

"I doubt that," Jessie said, stepping around him, blocking his way. She petted Donna, earning a tail wag and an affectionate nuzzle.

Traitor.

Erwin released a long sigh. "The woman was here one day. What could I have possibly done to change her entire life's trajectory? I might be a walking disaster, but I'm hardly apocalyptic."

Jessie smirked, her gaze landing on him. "You asked

the woman out before she'd had time to unpack. To the sunset stroll, no less. This is your fault."

Now, that was uncalled for. "I merely wanted to show her around town, help her get comfortable."

"Erwin, you don't have to pretend with me. You haven't been on a date in decades. You saw an available woman that was close to your age, and you went for it. She could have had a lump the size of Texas growing out of her right eye, and you'd still have asked her out."

Erwin's grip on the dog leash tightened, and he had to consciously loosen it. "You can't blame me, considering the slim pickings around here."

He tried to ignore Jessie's narrowed eyes and the hurt expression that flashed across her face. He knew that had been uncalled for. But sometimes she was so infuriating. It was like she went out of her way to make him miserable. Like her whole purpose in life was to remind him of what he'd had—and what he'd lost.

Jessie had the luxury to be able to move on with her life, tarts and baked goods in hand. Jessie was the mother of Starlight Ridge, the one who was beloved by all. Friends were never in short supply.

That was not Erwin's lot in life. No one invited him to social events, unless it was a town function. He didn't have friends. No one except Donna.

It was his fault, he knew.

Erwin could have been the guy that everyone enjoyed being around. He had been that person, many years ago.

He'd had the world in front of him—he could go anywhere, do anything, be anyone.

But he hadn't wanted to go anywhere outside Starlight Ridge. This was his home. And Jessie, the love of his life, had been here. Nothing else had mattered.

And then Jessie had left him.

Broken his heart.

And he hadn't been the same since.

Now, at sixty-one years old, he was still stuck in Starlight Ridge. And what did Erwin have to show for it?

A seafood restaurant. A saxophone. Donna.

And an ex-fiancée who just wouldn't leave him alone.

3

Jessie needed something to do. Someone to help. Maybe she'd make a pie for someone. Or volunteer at the library. They were short on funds since rebuilding and would probably appreciate someone doing story time.

Anything to distract herself from Erwin's bitter words.

But when Jessie stopped by the library, it was closed. According to a sign on the door, it didn't open until mid-afternoon because the new librarian, Eliza, had to work at the hardware store until three o'clock.

Okay. No worries. Adeline could probably use some company at the chocolate shop. Her husband, Eli, one of the most famous movie actors in the world, was gone for a couple of months. Italy, Jessie thought. Spain? Maybe Germany.

Jessie made the short walk to Starlight Chocolate

Confections and found Adeline behind the counter, boxing up her latest batch of truffles.

"Hey, Jess. What brings you in this morning?" Adeline asked, smiling when Jessie entered the shop. At least someone was happy to see her.

"Just thought I'd say hi," she said, making herself at home and slipping onto one of the barstools at the display counter. "Did you hear that Eliza was hired as the librarian? As much as I love the girl, I'm not sure the town council chose correctly. As a newlywed, she's always either with Travis or busy with the hardware store. She's still lifeguarding a couple of times a week too."

"They probably need the money. A little extra during the off-season never hurts." Adeline closed the lid on her last truffle box. "Need a little pick-me-up? I just finished a batch of caramels, your favorite."

Jessie smiled. She could always count on Adeline. "I never say no to your truffles."

"Speaking of what's new in town, how does Barbara seem to be settling in?"

So, Adeline hadn't heard.

Jessie prided herself on being kind and nonjudgmental, and always giving people the benefit of the doubt.

But how Barbara had treated Starlight Ridge after their generous hospitality—it made Jessie bristle just thinking about it.

Adeline had placed a couple of truffles on a small plate but paused. "What's wrong?"

"Nothing," Jessie said, attempting to bring back her smile. "Everything's fine. Barbara's fine. Probably. I wouldn't know because she left town in the dark of night, like a criminal. Couldn't handle our small-town hospitality. Or more likely, couldn't handle Erwin's advances. He scared her off, you know. Thought he'd ask out a woman he didn't know the first thing about. Like that's normal."

She knew she'd begun to spiral but didn't know how to stop herself. Not until Adeline placed a hand over Jessie's, her expression filled with concern.

"I'm sorry to hear that. I suppose even my truffles aren't enough to get some people to stay."

"Did you not hear the part about Erwin asking her out only a few hours after she arrived in town? I suppose he fancies himself some kind of geriatric Romeo. It backfired, of course. Sent the woman running as fast as she could manage."

Adeline's lips quirked up at the edges. "I'm sure he was charming, back in the day. Maybe he's just a little out of practice."

Jessie snorted. "Charming. Yes, I suppose he was, if you like that sort of thing." Unwanted memories washed over her. Images of moonlit strolls along the beach. Running into the waves, laughing. So much laughing. She shook herself from them. "I'll have you know, Addie, if that woman had tried even one of your truffles, she'd have dedicated her life to Starlight Ridge. Trust me, this fiasco is all on Erwin."

Adeline slid the plate of truffles over to Jessie. "When are you two going to decide that you would make better friends than enemies, huh? Aren't you tired of this feud of yours?"

If only it were that simple.

"It keeps life interesting. Keeps me from getting bored," Jessie said, biting into one of the truffles. Caramel oozed from the sides, and she closed her eyes, relishing it.

Didn't get much better than that.

Adeline choked on a laugh. "You? Bored? You're on every committee this town has, and some that don't technically exist. You're the town's most prolific matchmaker, and even though you sold your bakery a decade ago, you still bake out of your kitchen and provide the bed and breakfast with fresh tarts every morning. Let's not forget that you also exercise, never missing a day. You put us all to shame."

Yes, Jessie was aware of her bio.

"Things are slowing down, Addie," she said, playing with the remaining truffle. "Leanne has expanded her breakfast options for her guests at the bed and breakfast, so she only needs my tarts delivered twice a week now. Newcomers don't want welcome baskets. Our young people are leaving Starlight Ridge and not coming back. I've lived long enough that if there is something to do in this town, I've done it." Jessie lifted a shoulder. "Things are changing, and I'm unsure where I fit into it all."

Adeline placed a hand on her hip. "Is all this crazy talk just because a random woman you met yesterday decided she couldn't handle how delightful we all are? Jessie, you are the glue that holds this town together. You know everyone and everything about them. If someone is sick, you are the first person on their doorstep, a pot of soup in hand. If an eligible bachelor inadvertently stumbles into our little town, you have him engaged to be married by the end of the year. Without you, this town would grind to a halt."

Jessie's lips twitched up. It was totally true.

At least it had been.

"I don't know, Addie."

"I never thought I'd see the day when Jessie Carter didn't know what to do with herself. Not only that but feel sorry for herself."

Jessie's defenses immediately rose. "That's not fair. I'm grateful for my life—a life in which I have been amply blessed."

"And a life that has always revolved around other people. So what, Leanne doesn't need as many tarts and you don't have a new resident to welcome. When was the last time you did something for yourself?"

Jessie jutted out her chin. "Right now. I'm going to buy a box of chocolates from you. And then I'm going to eat them all. By myself."

Adeline smiled. "I believe that you'll buy a box. But I also know it will be empty by the time you get home. And not because you ate them. You'll offer one to every person you meet on your way."

It was the only way for Jessie to pretend that she wasn't alone.

"I won't offer one to Erwin."

That only made Adeline laugh. "Look. I'll make you a deal." She took a box of truffles from the pile next to her and slid it across the counter. "This box is for you—on the house. And there will be another just like it every week for the next month."

"What's the catch?" Jessie asked, suspicious. With Addie, you always had to be careful of the fine print.

Adeline's smile widened. "No catch. At least, nothing difficult. Each day, you'll wake up to a challenge that I've set."

"A challenge?" Jessie scrunched up her nose. That sounded purposely vague, and Adeline wasn't to be blindly trusted.

Adeline held up her hands in a defensive gesture. "I'm not trying to put one over on you. I'm not trying to be sneaky. One simple challenge that you have to complete each day. That's it."

Jessie folded her arms across her chest. "It feels like you're asking me to sell my soul to the devil for a box of chocolates."

Adeline might be as sweet as her truffles, but she was also devious.

"Look, you've done so much for the town over the last

few decades, I wanted to return the favor, if only in the limited way I know how." Jessie tried to interject that she really hadn't done all that much and no one owed her anything, but Adeline talked over her, speaking louder to drown Jessie out. "I'll even sweeten the deal. You do every challenge for the entire thirty days, and I'll teach you how to make my caramel truffles."

Jessie's words failed her, and she was sure she looked ridiculous, her mouth hanging wide open. "I've been begging you for that recipe for years," she finally said, her voice hoarse. "But I never actually expected you to hand it over. It's your trade secret. For all you know, I could open a competing chocolate shop next door, using your own recipe."

Adeline's eyes shined. She knew how much Jessie would love to have that recipe. It wasn't just the ability to have caramel truffles whenever she wanted. Jessie would be able to use the techniques and adapt them with her other signature baked goods.

"I'd be teaching you how to make one recipe, not the entire book," Adeline said, laughing. "Besides, it's the chile truffle recipe that I'll take to my grave."

Oh, yes. Adeline's signature.

Bree, over at the scuba shop, was originally from New Mexico and had insisted that Adeline was missing out by not including spicy chile chocolates in her shop. Addie had thought it was a terrible idea and had developed a recipe to prove it.

It had turned out to be her biggest seller. Go figure.

"This thirty-day challenge means that much to you?" What Jessie was really thinking was, *I mean that much to you*? Jessie was used to giving. She wasn't used to accepting. People had learned long ago to stop trying.

"Yes, it does," Adeline said. She seemed completely sincere.

But there was still something about it that made Jessie nervous. This was the woman who had snuck into her neighbor's apartment and hid an alarm clock underneath his bed—but not before setting it to play reggae music at full volume at three o'clock in the morning.

Jessie was getting too old for stuff like this.

Her lips quirked up into a smile. She knew that wasn't at all true.

She was the perfect age. And this was going to be fun.

4

Erwin scanned the contract for a third time. The lawyer was getting impatient. "Everything looks like it's in order. My legal counsel said there was nothing wrong with it—it's completely in my favor. With the exception that Seaside Bay will no longer be mine, of course." And that was the kicker. The reason why, despite knowing that this was the best deal he was ever going to get and he'd be crazy for not taking it, he couldn't get himself to sign.

Seaside Bay wouldn't be his.

Erwin had built the restaurant from the ground up. He'd run it seven days a week for the past twenty-eight years. He could count on one hand how many times he'd closed the restaurant for even a weekend.

He'd had to close it for a few days when it had flooded after a particularly bad storm. Then there was the time

Erwin had thrown an employee Christmas party and everyone got food poisoning because one of his waitresses had decided to bring a tainted seven-layer dip.

The most recent time—closed for a week after his mother died. It hadn't been long enough.

It wasn't like the restaurant was shutting its doors, though. It would live on. And Erwin wouldn't have to be the one there at eight o'clock each morning. And he could take vacations whenever he wanted. With the money he was being offered in this contract, he'd never have to worry about off-season again.

He could finally relax.

It sounded awful. But at his age, that was what people did. They started thinking about retirement. Traveling. Spending time with family.

Except, he didn't have much family left. His parents were gone. He'd had one younger brother and an older sister. His brother had passed away the previous year, and his sister had left home at the age of sixteen. He did manage to keep in touch with his brother's daughter. So, that was nice.

Erwin had never bothered to create a family of his own.

He'd thought about it, of course. Once. With a woman he'd been madly in love with. And she'd returned his love.

Until everything had gone terribly wrong.

"Mr. Anderson?" the lawyer said. He was looking pointedly at the contract.

Right.

"I'm going to need more time."

The lawyer's brow creased, and he stood. "My client won't wait much longer. He has his eye on several projects, and time is money."

Erwin had always found that to be an odd saying. He didn't agree that time was money.

Time was opportunity.

If you wanted to use that opportunity to make yourself more money, fine. But when you already had as much as the buyer obviously had, it seemed pointless to waste your time acquiring more.

He glanced out the restaurant window. His gaze landed on someone who was...well, there was no other way to say that they were acting like a crazy person. Running along the beach with their arms out like an airplane, splashing through the waves. The figure paused to pick up something from the beach, examine it, then throw it back into the ocean.

Jessie.

The woman was sixty years old, and she was out there acting like she was twelve.

He knew she'd been losing it, and he'd been warning town council for years, but this was the proof he'd needed. Where was his camera? He'd take a video, and finally they'd listen to reason. That spot as head of the welcoming committee was going to be his.

"Like I said, I'll need a little longer," Erwin said,

standing to match the lawyer. "Thanks for coming by. You'll have your answer soon."

The lawyer hesitated. "You won't get another offer like this. And I'm not just saying this because I represent my client's needs. This is a really good deal."

"It's a really good restaurant. Hate to see it go into the wrong hands. Never did trust an out-of-towner. Can't even be bothered to travel out here himself to talk things over with me."

The lawyer raised a shoulder, conceding the point. "Like I said, he's a busy man."

Erwin raised a hand in farewell, and the lawyer left.

He knew what needed to happen. Selling was the only reasonable thing to do at this point.

But he wasn't quite ready to take the plunge. A few more days. Then he'd sign.

On to more pressing matters. Blackmailing Jessie.

Erwin grabbed his video camera from the top of a bookshelf and hurried out to the deck that wrapped around the restaurant. It was October, so Starlight Ridge still had its warm days, but today was not one of those days. He wished he'd brought his jacket.

Jessie was wearing one, but it was drenched and probably doing more harm than good.

Now, how to work the camera. He rarely took pictures, let alone video. Had no need.

Erwin pressed a button that was obviously wrong because it brought up the settings menu instead.

It took another two wrong selections before he managed to start recording a video of his shoes. He lifted the camera, but it had taken so long, Jessie was no longer running through the waves. Instead, she stood on the beach, arms wrapped around her stomach. Even from that distance, Erwin could tell she was freezing.

Honestly, the woman had a death wish. Or was at least desperate to catch pneumonia. And at their age, it was practically the same thing.

Erwin muttered under his breath as he turned off the camera and hurried down a long set of stairs that would take him to the beach.

"Jessie, what on earth are you doing?" Erwin asked as he approached her. Now that he was closer, he could see that her lips were turning blue. "It's the coldest day we've had this month, and you decide to go for a swim?"

Jessie's lips tightened into a firm line. "I was reliving my childhood. And frankly, it was wonderful."

"Until you got wet and stopped moving long enough to realize how cold you are and that you have a mile-long walk back home?"

Jessie hesitated. "I don't think Adeline checked the weather before she gave me today's challenge. But nevertheless, day two is in the books. And it was a good one, if I say so myself."

Erwin cocked an eyebrow. "You jumped in the waves because Adeline challenged you to? Since when do we accept challenges from our dear chocolate shop owner? I'd thought you'd learned your lesson a long time ago."

"Never mind. You wouldn't understand." Jessie turned her back to him. "It's time I got home."

If Jessie left now, she would freeze to death before ever reaching the other side of town. Erwin and Jessie had their issues, but that didn't mean he wished ill on her.

"Come inside, Jess. Dry out. Then you can go home."

Jessie glanced over her shoulder and surprised him with a single bark of a laugh. "Don't feel like you have to be nice—chivalry isn't an obligation. At least not with me, it isn't."

Erwin frowned. "Fine. Freeze, then. But when Dr. Patty comes around here dragging your corpse behind her and asks why I let you walk home soaking wet, I'll be able to tell her that I tried. And that you were too stubborn to admit something as simple as the fact that you were cold. That you couldn't even accept a cup of hot chocolate before you wandered off to your death."

Jessie turned toward him and frowned. "Really? My corpse? That's a little extreme, even for you." But she brushed past him and started up the stairs toward Seaside Bay. "You never mentioned that hot chocolate was being offered."

Erwin watched as Jessie easily moved up the stairs, onto the deck, and in through the patio doors. He didn't know how she moved so quickly. It took him fifteen minutes each morning just to get his joints working properly.

He couldn't help but wonder, if they had followed through with their plan to get married all those years ago, would she have shared her secret? Would he also be able to take the stairs two at a time?

Didn't matter now. That was a long time ago.

So, he trudged after her in his usual way, having to hold onto the railing as he went.

Erwin hoped she would dry out quickly. The less time they spent together, the better.

5

J essie stepped into Seaside Bay, and her entire body prickled with relief as the warm air washed over her. Really, what had Adeline been thinking?

That it would be fun.

And, oh, it was.

Jessie hadn't had that much fun in a long time. She was sure she'd looked ridiculous, running along the sand and through the waves like that. But it hadn't mattered.

Because she'd felt free.

Giddy excitement settled over her as she wondered what adventure she might embark on the next day.

And then Erwin walked in, his breaths coming fast.

It startled Jessie.

This was a man she'd seen every day for decades, and yet she'd never stopped to really look at him.

It was too painful.

But she allowed herself to in that moment.

And she saw a man who had been tossed about by life.

It wasn't easy, relying on tourist season to get you through from one year to the next. And Erwin had placed himself at the forefront of everything, making sure the town, and everyone in it, got along as well as could be expected.

He'd dedicated himself to the town, and his restaurant.

This restaurant.

It had been what had started the downhill slide of her and Erwin's relationship all those years ago.

So, naturally, Jessie had never actually eaten at Seaside Bay. Never even gone inside.

She glanced around. It was nice, she supposed, if you were someone who enjoyed overt nautical themes, fishing nets decorating the walls, and a large swordfish hanging from the ceiling.

"You can sit anywhere," Erwin said, moving toward the back of the restaurant. "I'll prepare the hot chocolate. Still prefer caramel to hazelnut?"

It had been so long, Jessie hadn't thought about it. No one other than Erwin would have even known to ask. Funny that he'd remembered.

"Yes, I suppose I do."

Erwin gave her a funny look, like she should know if she enjoyed hazelnut, but merely grunted and disappeared around a corner.

Jessie unzipped her windbreaker and laid it out on a

table to dry, then slipped into the booth. Her jacket hadn't done much good. Every layer she wore was soaked. A large gas fireplace in the middle of the restaurant sat cold and empty. Not surprising, considering it was off-season. Many stores in Starlight Ridge closed up entirely from November through February. Not Erwin and his world-famous shrimp, though. This was his pride and joy.

When Erwin returned five minutes later, he held two steaming mugs.

The one he handed to Jessie had a small dollop of whipped cream on top. Just how she liked it. The other mug seemed to be nothing but whipped cream.

Erwin hesitated, like he was unsure if he was allowed to join her, or if it would be presumptuous to assume.

"Why don't you sit?" Jessie asked, fighting a smile. A chill ran through her, causing an involuntary shiver, and she wrapped her hands around the mug, soaking in its warmth.

Erwin's lips parted, and he quickly placed his hot chocolate on the table. "I should have turned on the fire. I didn't even think of it."

Jessie was about to protest, saying he needn't bother, that she wouldn't be staying long enough for him to go to the trouble. But he was already gone and turning on the gas before she had the chance.

As soon as the flames were going, though, she was glad for it. The heat from the fire was nearly instantaneous, and she relished it as she sipped her drink. Jessie released a satisfied sigh and leaned back in the booth.

"Thank you," she told Erwin when he returned.

He gave a grunt of acknowledgment and sat down, his pile of whipped cream in front of him.

"Why would you accept a challenge from Adeline?" Erwin asked after a prolonged silence. "You know how she is."

Jessie didn't know how to explain it in a way that Erwin would understand. If she told him she'd done it for a box of chocolates, he'd think she was out of her mind. If she told him it was for one of Adeline's secret recipes, he'd immediately tell her that Addie would never give up her recipe and that she was pulling some sort of prank on her.

Jessie could admit that was Addie's style. But not this time.

This time, it was because Adeline cared about Jessie. And apparently didn't trust Jessie to take care of herself.

Jessie should be offended, but Adeline wasn't completely off the mark.

Erwin wouldn't see it that way, though.

So Jessie instead asked, "When was the last time you ran in the waves?"

Erwin stared. "I don't run." He glanced at his watch. "I do, however, take Donna on walks. Three times a day. The second of which should have started twenty minutes ago. Donna will be prancing with worry."

Oh, yes. Erwin's beloved golden retriever. Jessie sometimes thought Donna was the only girl Erwin had ever had feelings for.

Herself included.

Erwin looked at his watch again, his brow creased in worry.

"Go," Jessie said. "Tell your waitress not to worry about me. I'll finish up my hot chocolate, then be out of her hair."

Erwin hesitated, and Jessie didn't understand what the problem was.

"What?"

Erwin seemed to make a decision and placed his hands on the table in front of him. "I can wait."

Jessie took a sip of her hot chocolate. It had reached the perfect temperature. "Why?"

"You are my guest."

Guest. That was one way of putting it. Jessie didn't understand Erwin at all. He spent most of his time avoiding her, but occasionally a switch flipped, and it was like he felt personally responsible for her.

It was the window shutters all over again. About ten years earlier, she'd discovered a broken shutter on her house, and she hadn't had the time or energy to deal with it. Erwin had shown up at her house one day, ladder in hand, and he'd spent hours fixing it.

He'd claimed he'd only done it because the noise of it banging against the house had been driving him crazy. And she could admit that it had tested her sanity.

But it wasn't like anyone else had offered.

Why Erwin?

"You offered to let me dry off inside your restaurant. I hardly think that makes you responsible for me. Go take care of Donna. I'll be fine."

Erwin didn't move.

Jessie rolled her eyes, picked up her mug, and chugged the rest. It was delicious—too bad it slid past her taste buds and straight down her throat, not giving her the opportunity to truly enjoy it. She set the mug down.

"Okay, let's go."

Erwin started. "Sorry?"

"Donna. She's waiting for you. Let's go get her."

He blinked a couple of times. "You're coming with me?"

"I have to go in that direction, anyway," Jessie said with a shrug. She was starting to dry off, so as long as she stayed away from the waves, she'd be fine.

Erwin stood. "Jess, I walk Donna alone. That's how it's been since she was a pup. Just her and me. It's our special time."

Of course it was.

Jessie released a long sigh. And the old Erwin was back.

"Well, you two have fun. I'm going to—"

Jessie didn't know what she was going to do with the rest of the day. She'd already baked the tarts and muffins for the bed and breakfast. She supposed she could see what Patty was up to at the medical clinic. Jessie hadn't had a checkup for a couple of months—wouldn't hurt to get another.

When Jessie didn't finish her sentence, Erwin raised a hand in farewell. "Whatever you do, don't go getting wet again. Maybe you should stop by Patty's on the way home. Just to get checked out for pneumonia or something like that. Can't be too careful."

Oh, darn. Now that Erwin had suggested she go to Patty's, she couldn't. Maybe she'd do that tomorrow.

"That's not how it works, Erwin."

He raised a shoulder like it didn't matter to him either way, then disappeared into the back of the restaurant, where the entrance to his upstairs apartment was.

"I can't believe I was going to marry that man," she muttered as she gathered up her windbreaker.

The waitress had just swung by to pick up her empty mug but stopped. "You and Mr. Anderson?" she said in awe, like she couldn't believe it either.

No one was supposed to know about that. Those who had been around back then had either been too young, or were now too old, to remember.

"Someone else," Jessie said, her words quick. Then she hurried out of the restaurant before she could be questioned further.

If only the memories could die as easily as their relationship had.

6

Erwin slammed his hands down on the rickety table in front of him. "No. We've had a traditional Thanksgiving dinner on the boardwalk every year since I was a kid, and we're not changing things up now."

"I'd hardly call it traditional," Patty said. "You think the Pilgrims had shrimp and salmon?"

"Not the point, and you know it." He held her gaze until she looked away.

"And now we're devolving into childlike tantrums," Jessie said wryly from the opposite side of the table. "Wouldn't be a town council meeting without it."

Erwin turned his narrowed eyes on her. He wasn't acting childish, he just had strong opinions. And he just so happened to be right. It wasn't his fault if they couldn't see it. "I don't hear you coming up with any solutions."

Jessie released a long sigh, like her patience couldn't

take much more. "You did hear them, but you didn't like them."

"We aren't doing a rotating dinner," Erwin said. "It's ridiculous."

"Only because you've never done one before," she said. "Our town is growing, and more people are staying. There isn't enough room for all of us to eat on the boardwalk at the same time. And if we have two rows of tables, we'll be so close together, we'll be eating off each other's laps. As much as I like Patty, I don't know if she'd appreciate that."

"Nope. I wouldn't," Patty agreed.

Jessie gave a curt nod, as if to say, *See, I told you so.*

"I like the rotating dinner idea," Bree said. "We have over a month to prepare and get the town used to the idea. We'd be happy to have one of the courses at the scuba shop. Right, honey?" She turned to her husband, Caleb, who sat next to her, bouncing their son on his lap.

Caleb looked surprised to have the attention suddenly on him, and Erwin could tell he had no idea what his wife had just asked him. Regardless, he nodded and said, "Sure. Sounds great."

Erwin snorted. "What exactly is a rotating dinner, Caleb?"

The scuba shop owner looked uncomfortable and glanced at his son, like he might be able to help. "Where... we rotate who gets dinner. We eat in shifts. And I call dibs on being in the first group."

Bree laughed and swatted her husband on the knee, as if he were making a joke.

Marriage was so nauseating.

"You'd think so," Erwin said. "But no. There would be seven locations, with seven different courses. Normally with a small group you'd start with appetizers and work your way up from there. But because this is an entire town we're talking about, we would all start on a different course. For example, heaven forbid, I could end up eating pie at the first stop, then proceed to the salad station, then the turkey, then the appetizers, and so on. Insanity is what it is."

"I think it could be fun," Jessie said.

"Of course you do."

Jessie leaned forward, her gaze boring into Erwin.

All he'd done was agree that she would think organized chaos was fun, but the way she was looking at him— maybe it had been his tone. He could admit that it had been sharper lately. Probably the stress of everything going on at the restaurant. And re-evaluating his life choices. Which was a bit difficult to do when you were sixty-one years old. That had led to its own frustrations.

"All I'm saying is that there has to be another option. Like maybe we can have two different sessions that people can sign up for. Similar to Caleb's version of the rotating dinner."

Jessie laughed, but it was devoid of humor. "Are you listening to yourself, Erwin? What happens if I end up in a different session than Leanne? I need her whipped yams. They are the only ones I'll eat."

"So make sure you sign up for the same session as her."

"But then Adeline might be in the other one. And you know I'm not missing out on her chocolate pie."

Erwin threw his arms into the air. "If dessert is the last stop on your rotating dinner, you still won't get any."

Jessie shook her head. "That's the beauty of it, Erwin. I'm on town council, and I get to be in any rotation I choose."

This was pointless.

"All in favor of having a rotating dinner where you might be eating your shrimp as dessert rather than an appetizer as it was intended, raise your hand," he grumbled.

Everyone raised their hands.

"Fine. This meeting is adjourned."

As Erwin gathered up his papers, Jessie approached him cautiously. "Look, Erwin, I know that vote didn't go the way you were hoping. But—"

"Jessie, whatever sage advice you are going to give me, please don't. I'm not in the mood."

She stopped and studied him. "Yes, I can see that. Trouble sleeping again? You know if you'd just try the tea I sent you—"

Erwin squeezed his eyes shut, his hands balling into fists. Deep breath. "I know you're trying to help, but there are some things that you can't fix. A rotating dinner is a new tradition to you, but to me it's just another thing that is changing. Another thing that will be unfamiliar. Another thing that I have to cope with. And I can't handle it right now."

And then he turned and walked away.

ERWIN REMOVED Donna's leash as soon as they reached the beach, allowing her to run as fast as her heart desired. Of course she immediately made a beeline for the waves, reminding him of Jessie's ludicrous behavior two days earlier.

She and Donna had much in common. They were both strong-willed. Independent. But wildly free and unconstrained.

Erwin knew that Jessie wouldn't take kindly to being compared to a dog. As loving and accepting as Jessie was with everyone around her, she was not fond of the four-legged creature. So, of course the first thing he'd done after they'd broken up was gone out and gotten one.

It hadn't been Donna, of course. She was the fourth dog Erwin had had since then.

But Donna was his favorite.

Of course, she still had her moments. Like now. After running in the waves, getting as wet as possible, Donna had decided it would be a good idea to roll around in the sand.

"Come on. What are you doing to me here?" he asked, helplessly watching from afar.

But that was life, wasn't it? Things could sneak up on you—blindside you.

And suddenly you found yourself staring at a contract, considering selling your life's work, because of a blood test. An anomaly.

Or in Patty's words...old age.

But if Erwin didn't have his restaurant, what did he have left?

Nothing.

Erwin bent down to pet Donna as she raced toward him but realized a moment too late what her plan was. Donna skidded to a stop and shook herself, sand and water spraying everywhere. And then she sat perfectly still, looking up at him with her wide brown eyes, as if she expected to be rewarded.

"You think you can get away with that, do you?" he asked, releasing a small chuckle. He took her favorite ball out of a small backpack and threw it as far down the beach as he could. She took off, chasing it, spraying more sand as she ran.

Erwin's gaze traveled over the water and out to where it met the sky.

There was a big world out there—a world he'd never explored. Never cared to.

But with the sale of the restaurant, there'd be nothing

keeping him in Starlight Ridge. He could travel anywhere he liked, as often as he liked.

Maybe if he had someone to share it with.

But he was afraid that ship had sailed, and it wasn't ever returning to harbor.

Unless…

No, that was a terrible idea. Worst one he'd had in decades.

That didn't keep him from mulling it over, though. Wondering.

And then finally putting a plan in place.

But even then, he was unsure if he'd actually go through with it.

7

J essie's eyes flew open. Light was streaming through the cracks in her blinds. She glanced at the alarm clock.

Six-thirty.

She jumped out of bed, slipped into her robe, and hurried downstairs, taking the steps two at a time.

Jessie didn't used to be quite so excited for the day to start. She'd never dreaded it, by any means, but now—there was a new excitement that permeated each day. A curiosity.

What challenge would Adeline leave on Jessie's porch today?

With each card Jessie found on her porch, she'd discovered a new excitement for life. The previous day she'd eaten breakfast for dinner, something she hadn't done in decades, and of course she'd invited several friends over.

Because who wanted to eat breakfast for dinner by themselves?

Chocolate chip pancakes, sausage, fresh-cut fruit, bacon, hashbrowns, and of course Jessie's world-famous fruit tarts—Jessie had gone all out. She'd even told her friends to come in their pajamas, and then they'd played board games long into the night.

Jessie had been missing that kind of spontaneity in her life.

It was difficult to find, when all her friends in town were at least twenty years younger and had families. They couldn't just drop everything and hurry out to her house whenever she had a crazy idea.

Except last night. Last night, they'd done just that. She'd told them not to worry about babysitters, and they'd all shown up on her porch with their kids. She'd felt like the grandmother she'd never become, her home full of food and children and laughter.

Jessie beat back the feeling of disappointment—the feeling that she'd missed out on something in her life. Something important.

But whether or not she had family by blood, this town was her family. And last night was evidence of that.

Jessie swung the front door open, the cold air attacking her, replacing the warmth inside. She relished it as it awakened her senses, her vision suddenly sharper, her hearing crisper. She pulled in a long breath, then looked for the familiar envelope.

There it was. Even on a Saturday, before the town had a chance to realize that morning had arrived, the envelope awaited her. The design was always the same—blue, white, and gold plaid, with her name written in cursive. As if anyone else could mistake the card as theirs.

But today was different. It sat on a box of caramel truffles.

Jessie had completed her first week.

And truffles for breakfast seemed exactly like the kind of thing that would be in keeping with the spirit of the challenges.

Jessie picked up the truffles and card and brought them inside.

She hummed a song to herself as she retrieved a letter opener to unseal the card. It was a tune she knew well but couldn't for the life of her remember the name of or even where she'd heard it.

It turned out that the chocolates weren't the only thing that made today's challenge different.

Normally there were specific instructions on what Jessie was to do that day. Play in the ocean. Make breakfast for dinner. Have a dance party.

Today's instructions consisted of only two words.

Say Yes.

Okay. But say yes to what?

"Yes," Jessie said aloud, feeling a bit ridiculous after doing so.

Nothing happened. No one popped out of hiding,

informing her that she'd said the magic words and now something spectacular was going to happen.

It was just Jessie, alone in her kitchen, talking to herself.

She flipped the card over. It was blank. When she turned it back, she noticed small print on the very bottom. The print was so small, she had to retrieve her reading glasses to decipher what it said.

To Everything, All Day.

Say yes to everything, all day.

That was a bit more ominous than the other challenges, and certainly right up Adeline's alley. She was the type who would tell others in town to approach Jessie and request random things, just to see what she would do.

Jessie was suddenly nervous about leaving the comfort of her home, unsure what awaited her. She assumed that a giant chicken costume would surface as some point, payback for when Jessie had required the same thing of Adeline a couple of years earlier.

In all fairness, Adeline had agreed to the terms of their friendly competition, and the consequence had been fair.

That wouldn't stop her from seeking retaliation, though. Even if that chicken costume had been one of the catalysts that led to Adeline marrying her movie star husband.

Jessie opened the box of truffles and popped one into her mouth, chewing slowly. Yes, she could hide inside for the rest of the day, but that would defeat the purpose of this challenge. Rather than feeling young and alive and happy, Jessie would be alone and miserable. She wasn't meant to stay indoors. Never had been.

So, after Jessie's breakfast of truffles and leftover pancakes, she dressed in the brightest, most fun outfit she could find (yellow with sunflowers on it—people would be able to spot her a mile away).

And she left the house.

Surprisingly, nothing happened.

No one was waiting to accost her with some ridiculous request. There was no chicken costume. Just a crisp fall morning with beautiful blue skies and the sound of the ocean waves crashing against the beach in the distance.

It was perfect.

And instead of thinking defensively, Jessie was now on the offensive. Where could she go where she was sure to find something she'd love to say yes to?

The scuba shop. As soon as Jessie entered, Bree would invite her to go for a walk down to the beach with her and her young son, who was always getting into mischief. It was easier for Bree to slip away during the off-season because her husband, Caleb, didn't do scuba lessons and could watch the shop.

When Jessie reached the back of the shop and rang the doorbell, however, Bree called down from their second-floor window, informing her that their entire family had come down with the flu.

There would be no morning beach walks with Bree and little Monty after all.

"But since you're here, maybe you could pick up some medicine for us from the market?" Bree asked.

Jessie grinned. "Yes," she called up.

That little word felt so powerful today. Like anything was possible with those three letters. Jessie hurried up the hill to Mueller Market and came back with not only medicine, but also soda, saltine crackers, soup, and a small stuffed bear.

Mission accomplished.

Now what?

Jessie decided she'd still like that morning walk, even if she'd need to do it alone, and turned her attention across the street. Isaac sat on his perch, gaze sweeping the empty beach. Not much for a lifeguard to do during off-season, but the ocean was his happy place.

She made her way to his station and tapped the side of his seat, startling him. "You're looking good up there," she said.

"Jessie, you can't scare a guy like that," Isaac said, a hand over his heart as he laughed. It was cold enough that he was actually wearing a shirt, but it wasn't enough to conceal that he was still the suntanned surfer their town all knew and loved.

"Sorry, didn't mean to. Everyone seems to be inside today, staying warm, so I thought I'd stop by and say hi. Do you really need to be out here if no one is swimming?"

Isaac was already nodding like he'd heard the question a thousand times before. "If it can prevent even one accident, I'm happy to be out here. It's the job I was hired to do. Besides, sometimes I need some space to think—and what better place than this?" He raised his arms and moved them in a circle, indicating the entire ocean in front of him.

'Don't I know it." Jessie paused. "I was more thinking about Leanne's perspective. Now that her folks have retired, the bed and breakfast is a big place for you two to take care of on your own. Especially since you work the beach part-time, and she's still writing screenplays."

Isaac waved a hand in the air. "Running the bed and breakfast isn't too much at all. Leanne writes her screenplays during the off-season and hires help during tourist season. We both get our surfing in first thing in the morning, and that sets us up for whatever challenges the day presents."

But then his face slackened, like he'd just realized something. "I forgot to stop by the new Italian bistro. Leanne asked if I could swing by on my way to the beach and place a catering order." He glanced at his phone. "It has to be in by ten or they won't be able to have it done in time. That's in twenty minutes. Leanne's going to kill me."

So much for handling everything.

"Do you want me to go for you? I don't mind."

Isaac shook his head. "Thanks, Jess, but it's kind of a complicated order. This group has a lot of allergies, which is why we're having their meals catered." He paused, and his expression brightened, like he'd just had an idea. "Will you watch the beach for me? It won't be for very long. I'll just run up, submit the order, and run back."

Jessie eyed the beach warily, as if a family reunion was suddenly going to show up with fifteen kids in tow. "You can't just leave it for twenty minutes? I'm sure no one would mind—"

"If anything happened while I was gone, it would be my fault," he interrupted. "Please."

Jessie squeezed her eyes shut. "Yes. I'll help you out. Just...be quick."

Because if anything happened while he was gone, regardless if he was blamed for leaving his post, she would always know that it had been she who had let the town down.

"You're the best," Isaac said, leaping from the life-guarding station. He tore his whistle off over his head and placed it around Jessie's neck. "You see anything suspicious, you just blow that and I'll come running."

Jessie nodded slowly and plastered on a smile. So what, she hadn't swum in years and would be worse than useless in an emergency. It would be fine. No one was at the beach. It would all be okay.

And then Isaac was off running toward the boardwalk, checking his phone as he went.

Well, it could be worse. If she was going to be taking over for Isaac for the next little while, that meant she also got to sit at his post.

And she didn't mind that one bit.

Jessie smiled as she climbed the ladder to where Isaac usually sat, overlooking everything. It was amazing how far she could see, despite being only six feet off the ground. No wonder Isaac didn't want to give up his life-guarding position—this was something she could get used to.

Too bad she'd make a terrible lifeguard, considering she didn't know CPR and couldn't swim to save her own life, let alone someone else's. It hadn't always been that way—she'd been quite good at it when she was younger. But things changed—life got in the way. She hadn't even attempted to swim in at least a decade.

Who knew, maybe she was still good at it and didn't even realize.

With how cold the weather had turned, today wasn't the day to test her abilities. Knowing her luck, she'd get halfway out and her body would shut down, and that would be the end of Jessie Carter.

So instead, she settled back in the chair, her gaze scan-ning the beach and a slight smile playing on her lips. She'd enjoy this while she could.

And then her gaze landed on a man walking along the beach in the distance. Her pulse quickened. Didn't look like he had any interest in swimming, so she didn't think she'd need to worry about blowing the whistle, or worse, attempting to save him herself.

The figure carried flowers, but at that distance, she still

couldn't tell who it was. Maybe Caleb was surprising Bree. It seemed like the kind of thing he would do.

Jessie was happy for whoever it was. She had spent most of her life helping people find moments like these.

But as the figure turned and worked his way toward the boardwalk, bitter disappointment was left in his wake.

She had recently had her sixtieth birthday and was now past hope she'd ever have one of those moments herself.

Her gaze returned to the view in front of her.

At least she had the ocean. And this town.

The rest of it—she pretended it didn't matter.

Until she arrived home thirty minutes later and discovered a bouquet of beautiful flowers sitting on her porch.

Now, nothing else mattered.

8

F lowers.

On her doorstep.

That couldn't be right.

Jessie inched forward, as if they would disappear if she moved too quickly.

But they didn't disappear, and instead looked more vibrant than ever. What an unusual color combination. Bright oranges and pinks contrasted with the green.

They were the kind of flowers Jessie would pick out for herself.

Jessie knelt next to the bouquet, still not daring to lift it. A card sat nestled in the leaves.

This had to be a mistake.

She kept telling herself that, even as she read her name, scrawled on the outside of the envelope.

Jessie knew that handwriting. It had been a long time since she'd seen her name written in it, though.

Erwin.

But that didn't make sense. The most she could expect from the man most days was a grunt as they crossed paths, and even then, he usually went out of his way to avoid her.

You'd think that after thirty years, he'd have forgiven her for breaking off their engagement.

Even after all this time, Jessie didn't regret it. It had been the right decision. She'd thought.

But looking down at the flowers, she was suddenly unsure.

Either way, there was no use letting them die outside in the cold. Jessie picked up the bouquet and brought it inside, snipping off the ends of the stems and placing them in water.

She picked up the card from where she'd set it on the counter. It had the insignia from Natalie's florist shop just down the street. Erwin had been approaching from the opposite direction, though. Jessie wondered how long he'd been wandering around town before he'd finally ended up at her place.

Jessie slipped the card out of the envelope.

Had a lot on my mind the past few days. Meet me for dinner tonight? 5:30 at Mitch's Place. I know you like to eat early.

Erwin

Jessie smirked. Erwin could pretend he'd chosen an early

dinner time for her, but she knew for a fact that he started getting ready for bed as soon as the sunset stroll finished. And this time of year, that was usually around seven-thirty.

Of course, Jessie couldn't deny enjoying an early bedtime as well. It wasn't like there was anything to do once the sun went down, and it made getting up in the morning easier.

And then the gravity of what had happened settled over her.

Erwin was asking her out on a date. Or to dinner, which was practically the same thing. Erwin hadn't asked Jessie to spend time with him in thirty years. And certainly hadn't given her flowers.

Her heart quickened, and she had to sit down.

Why now?

It didn't really matter why. Because she couldn't go.

Jessie had always said that it was Erwin who had made things weird between them. It had been him who had avoided her, not the other way around.

But the way her breathing had shallowed at the thought of seeing Erwin outside of a town council meeting. Outside of the occasional run-in. Purposely going to where he was. Sitting with him. Pretending that was normal.

She knew it hadn't been just him who had avoided the other—who had made things weird.

And she was angry. Why would Erwin try to change things up now? Why couldn't they just stick with the status quo? It had taken them long enough to get to this point, and now he was messing with it.

Jessie glanced at her watch. Two-thirty.

That gave her enough time to call Seaside Bay and tell Erwin that she wasn't going to be at dinner. The phone call would be awkward, but not as awkward as actually attending.

She tossed the card onto the table, and it landed right next to Adeline's.

The challenge.

The recipe.

If Jessie wanted it, she had to say yes to everything today.

She had the uneasy feeling that Adeline had known Erwin was going to pull something like this. Or maybe Erwin and Adeline had planned it together.

Jessie knew it was unlikely as soon as she thought it. Erwin didn't hatch plans. And he'd certainly not make Adeline privy to what he was up to.

This challenge was no longer as fun as it had been.

But Jessie knew what she needed to do.

She needed to go out to dinner with Erwin.

Her ex-fiancé.

The man who had broken her heart.

JESSIE DIDN'T CALL ERWIN—DIDN'T tell him that she was going to accept his invitation. She wanted to leave her options open until the last possible moment.

It was tempting to not show up. Adeline didn't know about the dinner date. Jessie could still claim she'd completed the day's challenge.

But she wasn't that kind of person. She couldn't lead Adeline, her friend, to believe something that wasn't true. The guilt would consume her.

Besides, Jessie was deluding herself if she thought Adeline wouldn't find out. She always did.

So, here she was. Walking into Mitch's Place, a high-end burger restaurant.

Jessie's gaze took in the empty tables. Such was off-season. Like most of the restaurants in Starlight Ridge, Mitch's would be closing up for the winter in the next month or so.

"Hey, Jess. I don't see you here often," Jules said, walking up with a menu. "You here alone?"

Jessie hesitated. Her feud with Erwin was well known in town, and she'd rather people not know she'd gone out to dinner with him. The appetite for gossip and speculation was insatiable, especially when business was slow and people didn't have anything else to occupy their attention.

"She's here with me," Erwin said, walking up behind her. "My usual table, please."

If Jules was surprised, she didn't show it. She'd likely had a lot of experience with unusual circumstances, considering that when she wasn't waitressing, she was working at the bed and breakfast. They'd had their fair share of celebrities stay there, and who knew what she'd come across with that bunch.

Jules led them to a booth that sat along the far wall and laid the menus down. "Anything to drink?"

"Water for me," Jessie said. "Lemon wedges as well, please."

"Water for me. No lemon," Erwin said.

Jessie fought a smile. The man had never liked lemon in any form. Lemonade. Lemon candy. She'd thought she'd finally convert him one year by convincing him to try her lemon bars, but that had only resulted in a lot of dry heaving and a deeper conviction that everything lemon was evil.

Jessie had thought that a bit dramatic. Her lemon bars had won first place at the county fair, after all. Even so, she hadn't dared try to get Erwin to consume anything lemon-flavored since.

"It's been a while since I've been here," Jessie said once Jules left to get their waters. "I like what Mitch has done with the place." Truth be told, it didn't look the least bit different from when Jessie had been there several months earlier, but when she was nervous, she just said the first thing that came to mind. And apparently the only thing she could think to comment on was Mitch's interior decorating skills.

It didn't used to be that way. She and Erwin—people wouldn't believe it if she told them—used to make each other laugh until they cried.

They might believe it of Jessie, but time hadn't been kind to Erwin. Somewhere along the way, he'd lost his spark. His excitement for life.

Jessie didn't know the last time she'd seen Erwin smile, let alone laugh.

So, what was she doing there?

Erwin glanced around the restaurant. "Yes, he's done well for himself. Not as well as Seaside Bay, of course. But not bad."

And there it was. Having to sneak in how well his restaurant was doing, while she'd sold her business years earlier. Always a competition. A quest to prove that he'd been right and she'd been wrong.

"No restaurant will ever compare to Seaside Bay, will it?" Jessie said, attempting to keep the bitterness out of her voice but not quite succeeding.

Erwin seemed surprised by the comment. "I wasn't saying my restaurant was better—"

"That's exactly what you were saying," Jessie said, interrupting. "And yet, you have a 'usual table' here. Which means you come here quite a lot. So, why do you have to compare the two? I'll tell you why. Because you want to rub Seaside Bay's success in my face. I chose to sell my bakery, you know. Not because I had to. Or the food wasn't good. Or people had stopped coming. I received petitions after selling it to Adeline, begging me to reopen. Telling me that my bakery was a staple of Starlight Ridge and that it had been a crime, closing the way I had. It's the reason I now have a home business and sell from my kitchen. Because I was good at what I did. Successful. So successful, in fact, that I was too busy. Wasn't having fun anymore. And I was able to retire early."

Jessie stopped, sucking in a deep breath. Erwin hadn't mentioned her bakery. Hadn't even alluded to it.

But there it was. All that pent-up frustration. Words that had been left unspoken for so long.

Erwin stared, speechless. Jules returned with their waters and asked if they were ready to order.

Jessie couldn't do this. Couldn't have dinner with Erwin, pretending everything was okay. She managed to be civil in their day-to-day interactions. Mostly. But this... This was too much.

"I think I should go," Jessie said, standing to leave.

"No," Erwin said, jumping up. "Please. Just eat with me. This one time. Hear what I have to say."

Jessie hesitated. And not only because her challenge had been to say yes to everything all day. But also because of the earnestness that lay behind Erwin's eyes. The intensity of it.

She slowly sat down. "Okay. If it's that important to you."

Erwin nodded to poor Jules, who seemed unsure what was happening and if she was meant to stay or go. "I'll have the barbecue burger, thank you. No fries. Steamed vegetables instead."

"Since when are you against french fries?" Jessie asked,

settling back into her seat. "You used to live off the things."

Erwin's lips twitched up slightly at one edge. Not quite a smile. But closer than Jessie had seen in a long time. "Which is why I can't have them anymore. Apparently, I'm getting old. Or so Patty seems to think."

Jessie released a long sigh. "Ah, yes. She told me the same thing at my appointment. But it was more in surprise, because she says I have the body composition of someone much younger. A decade, at least."

The almost-smile disappeared.

Why did Jessie have to say things like that? Even though it was true, she'd known she was saying it just to one-up him.

She turned to Jules. "I'll have the jalapeño burger, please. And the steamed vegetable in lieu of fries as well." They handed the menus to Jules, and she disappeared, like she couldn't get out of there fast enough.

"I didn't come here to fight," Erwin said.

Jessie nodded slowly. "I know. Old habits."

"We didn't used to fight."

Jessie played with the silverware that sat in front of her wrapped in a linen napkin. She spun the bundle first one way, then the other. "That was a long time ago, Erwin. I hardly remember the days when we didn't fight. Now, it's all about town council, ordinances, and if we can all fit on the boardwalk for Thanksgiving."

Erwin was quiet, and Jessie sneaked a glance at him. He was watching her, thoughtful. His expression softened as he said, "I remember driving down to Turtle Bay in the middle of the night, just the two of us. You'd been saying we weren't able to see each other nearly enough because we were always working. You were right, of course. It was tourist season, so you know how that goes."

Memories flooded Jessie, and she wished there was some way to stop them. "You knocked on my door at two in the morning like a crazy person."

"I couldn't sleep," Erwin said, raising a shoulder in concession. "I told you that you were right. We didn't see each other nearly enough. And I asked you to get dressed. We drove down to Turtle Bay with no light but the moon and stars. Didn't have cell phones back then."

"Or apparently flashlights," Jessie said with a small chuckle. "I came away from the excursion with so many scrapes that people thought I'd been attacked."

Erwin laughed. "But it had also been the best night of my life. We were so tired, we could barely function at work the next day. But it had been worth it."

Jessie started at Erwin's laugh. She hadn't realized how much she'd missed it. Not only hearing him laugh but being the reason behind it.

"Erwin, what am I doing here?" Jessie asked, her voice soft.

Erwin shifted in his seat, like he was uncomfortable, but he then suddenly sat up straight and looked Jessie in the eyes.

"I want to court you. Again. I want to get married."

9

E rwin's hands were sweating so profusely, he had to hide them under the table and wipe them on his pants. Multiple times.

He hadn't meant for it to come out like that. The plan had been to bring up several more wonderful memories. Then ask if she'd consider going out with him. On dates. Just to get to know each other again.

Yes, he'd considered the eventual possibility of marrying Jessie. But he wasn't supposed to bring that up for a very long time. And certainly not tonight.

But now that he'd brought it up, he'd have to run with it.

"Like it or not, time is running out," Erwin said. "We're not getting any younger, and I'm old enough to have a lot of regrets. Too many to be comfortable with. When I had my yearly appointment with Patty, it reminded me of my fragility. And how much time I've lost. How much has been wasted." He pulled in a long breath. "I know I push everyone away. That I'm stubborn. And ornery. And that people don't like me much."

Erwin paused and squeezed his eyes shut. He hadn't meant to mention all of that either. They certainly weren't selling points. When had he become such a mess?

He already knew the answer to that.

The day Jessie left.

"The point is," Erwin said, "the only life worth living is with you. And everything else that has happened between us—I want to make up for it. I want to show you that just because we lost out on the last three decades doesn't mean we need to lose out on the next three."

Of course, that would put them at ninety years old, but who knew, it could happen. At this point, it was less about the math and more about getting Jessie to at least consider a future with him.

Jessie was quiet. More like stunned.

Erwin hoped he hadn't come across as too desperate.

He thought back to the past five minutes.

Definitely desperate.

But maybe it was an endearing desperation, as opposed to a run-and-hide kind of desperation.

"You're right," Jessie said slowly. "We're not getting any younger. But that doesn't mean we can pretend our lives didn't play out the way they did. There was a reason that things ended the way they did with us. It took ten years for us to even be in the same room together. Another ten for us to be able to have a conversation. We can't pretend that didn't happen."

"But look at us now," Erwin said, a hopeful lilt to his voice.

Jessie gave him a sad smile. One full of pity. "Yes, look at us. It took us thirty years to be able to sit down and have a meal together. We're not exactly marriage material, Erwin. I don't think we were marriage material thirty years ago, either. The ending to our relationship was always there, always lurking. Of course, I don't think anyone could have anticipated the spectacular way it would come about —akin to an atomic bomb."

Erwin was already shaking his head. "No. I don't accept that. We were meant to be together."

Jessie hesitated, then reached across the table, resting a hand on Erwin's forearm. "I'm sorry, Erwin. I can't marry you."

The words cut Erwin, and he struggled to breathe. At least Jessie didn't look pleased at having to say them. In fact, she looked like she was going to be sick. But she didn't take them back. Instead, they seemed to strengthen her resolve.

The food arrived shortly after, and they finished their meal in pained silence.

There was nothing left to say.

That wasn't true. There was one more thing he needed to get off his chest.

"I was wrong to not support you opening your bakery," Erwin said, pushing his empty plate away from him. "I acted like my idea was the only good one. Didn't even consider your perspective. I was the man, and I was going to provide for my family. And in my mind, there was only one way to do that. In Starlight Ridge, that meant opening a business. But it couldn't be just any business. It had to be my business. And that wasn't fair to you. You didn't feel listened to, because you weren't. And I am sorry for that."

Jessie moved the last piece of broccoli around on her plate. "All I wanted to do was bake. And I was good at it."

"I know. And I couldn't tell the difference between baking and cooking. Told you that you could work in the kitchen at Seaside Bay. Never mind that despite liking fish, you hate the smell of it. That was on me. And I own it."

Erwin could tell he was losing her. That Jessie had forgotten the good memories. That they'd gotten lost in everything that had happened after.

He'd had the idea of opening Seaside Bay. She'd wanted to open a bakery. They hadn't had the resources to open both. And neither of them had budged. They'd each had a vision, and because neither of them was willing to compromise, they'd gone their separate ways, each intent on proving the other wrong. Intent on showing that their idea had been the better one.

And they'd been at odds ever since.

Of course, that was the nice way of putting it.

Going their separate ways had actually meant bringing

their argument to a town meeting and asking residents which restaurant they'd prefer. When their neighbors refused to vote on it, things had escalated. Quickly.

No one in town ever spoke of that day. But no one had forgotten.

Thankfully, most of the current residents of Starlight Ridge hadn't been there thirty years ago.

"Things did not end well, Erwin. And I appreciate the apology. But it's thirty years too late." Jessie stood. "Thank you for dinner. It was delicious. But no more flowers. No more invitations."

"We were meant to be together," Erwin said again, hating how panicked he sounded. "Have you ever stopped to ask yourself why neither of us ever married?"

Jessie shook her head. "It's because we broke each other, Erwin. That doesn't mean we were meant to be together—it means we were so terrible for each other that we are beyond repair." She slung her purse over one shoulder. "I made it my life's mission to help others find what I never did. Because I still believe in love. And I believe in happily-ever-after. But not for me. And certainly not for us. I'm sorry."

Erwin watched as Jessie walked out of the restaurant. She never looked back.

10

J essie didn't know where to go.

Not the beach, where people were gathering for the sunset stroll.

She fumed as she walked, furious with herself for going to dinner. It hadn't mattered what Erwin wanted; she'd known it would end badly. But she'd said yes because of Adeline's stupid challenge.

Didn't matter now, because Jessie had said no to his proposal.

She'd lost the challenge.

But Addie's caramel truffle recipe was not worth agreeing to date Erwin—to marry him.

That ship had sailed a long time ago.

Specifically, when they had been throwing insults at each other in that town meeting.

It had been ugly. And unlike them.

Gone were the two young people, so deeply in love they'd have done anything for each other. They'd been like Isaac and Leanne...dating from when they'd been teenagers.

It hadn't ever been a question of if they'd get married, but when.

And then it had all ended in an explosion of awfulness.

Things had been said that couldn't be taken back.

Unlike Isaac and Leanne, Jessie and Erwin hadn't ever been able to find their way back to each other.

And that was how it was.

No matter how much Erwin was feeling his age and regretting what had been, it was done.

Jessie attempted to think of anything but him as she wandered the streets, not wanting to go home.

The flowers were still there. A reminder of a love that had died long ago but was not forgotten.

At least he'd apologized. That was more than she'd ever gotten from him after their disastrous ending.

All over whether they were going to open a seafood restaurant or a bakery.

And Jessie had hated Seaside Bay ever since.

Because it had ended a seven-year courtship.

Jessie slapped away a few stray tears. She hadn't cried over Erwin for a very long time, and she wasn't about to start now. She paused, glancing around.

She was on the backside of Adeline's chocolate shop.

Of course she was.

Guilt gnawed at Jessie. She needed to tell Adeline the challenge was off.

Jessie hesitated at the back door, confident that Adeline would be down at the sunset stroll. Or at home. She knocked anyway.

Adeline answered. She wore an apron and had chocolate streaks on her forehead. "Jessie," she said, her eyebrows popping up in surprise. "What are you doing here?"

"You're working awfully late, aren't you?" Jessie said, circumventing the question. "It's not tourist season, you know. You're supposed to be relaxing a bit."

Adeline laughed and opened the door wider so that Jessie could enter. "I know, but Eli arrives home tomorrow, and I want to spend as much time with him as I can. I've been working all day so I don't have to come in early for the rest of the week."

Young love. Envy took hold, but Jessie smothered it just as quickly.

"I can admit that Starlight Ridge isn't the same while he's away," Jessie said with a smile.

Adeline led Jessie into the back kitchen. "I know what you mean. He has a vibrancy about him that is difficult to replace." She spun to face Jessie. "But you didn't stop by to chat about how wonderful my husband is. How did the challenge go today?"

Jessie's gaze dropped. "I'm out. I couldn't do it."

Adeline didn't respond, and when Jessie looked up, she

saw that Adeline was watching her with sympathetic eyes. "What happened? I thought this one would be easy for you."

Jessie nodded. "It was. At first. Even got to have life-guarding duty for a bit. I can see why Isaac likes it so much."

"And then?" Adeline prodded.

Jessie couldn't bring herself to say the next part aloud. It was embarrassing. A sixty-year-old woman being asked out on a date by her ex-fiancé. It was ridiculous. A young person problem.

"I saw Erwin walk past here holding flowers," Adeline said. "Were those for you or another woman?"

After Erwin had turned from the beach and toward the boardwalk, he'd have had to pass Adeline's store. Jessie wondered how many other people had noticed.

"Me," Jessie admitted.

"We thought so. And about time too." Adeline gave a satisfied nod. But then she hesitated, like that might not have been the right thing to say.

"What do you mean by 'We thought so'? Who else saw him?"

Adeline's cheeks reddened. "Just...a few people. Who happened to be out and about. And I might have done some digging, calling Natalie's florist shop. Don't worry, she wouldn't tell me a thing. Said she'd been sworn to secrecy. But she may have had a couple of customers at the time who had overheard the conversation."

Jessie's heart dropped. "You mean, the entire town knows."

"Something like that." At least Adeline had the decency to act embarrassed, but she didn't act surprised. It was as if she'd known that Jessie and Erwin had a past.

"You know we were engaged. Way back when."

A nod.

"And the rest of the town?" Jessie already knew the answer before Adeline confirmed Jessie's suspicion. Everyone knew, and probably had for years, but never said anything.

Because they were kind. And they were family. And judging by Adeline's reaction to the news, they'd apparently been hoping that Erwin and Jessie might one day rekindle their flame.

Jessie raised a shoulder and turned to leave, because there was nothing left to say.

"This doesn't mean you forfeit the challenge," Adeline said. "I'll give you a pass. Contrary to what you might believe, I had no idea that Erwin was planning that for today."

Jessie glanced back. "You don't need to do that. I didn't follow through with the challenge. Fair and square." She paused. "For the record, I did say yes when he asked me to go out to dinner with him. But what he asked me next... Even your truffle recipe wasn't enough for me to agree to his request."

Adeline hurried around Jessie, forcing her to face her.

"You went out to dinner with Erwin. Because you didn't want to lose my challenge?"

Jessie nodded.

Adeline disappeared into the back, then reappeared a moment later holding a piece of paper. She waved it in the air. "This is my recipe. You deserve it."

"But I didn't do the full thirty days," Jessie protested.

"Doesn't matter. You went out to dinner with Erwin Anderson. And both of you walked away alive and unharmed. I've seen you two in town meetings together, and like I said, you deserve this."

Adeline extended the recipe toward Jessie, but she didn't take it.

"He asked me to marry him, Addie. Said he was sorry for everything that happened all those years ago. From what I can tell, he's panicking about the fact that he's getting old, and he doesn't feel like he has much to show for it. Feels like life has passed him by. And he's trying to make himself feel better by getting me to forgive him. Marry him. Make up for lost time."

Adeline's expression slackened, and Jessie wondered if she'd need to get a forklift to pick Addie's jaw off the floor. "No wonder you couldn't stick to the challenge," she finally said. "What was the man thinking? He knows that's not how relationships work, right? You can't be at odds with your ex-fiancée for decades and then expect to pick up where you left off. Especially considering that you nearly ruptured eardrums with how loud things got between you two."

Apparently, everyone knew the entire story, even the ones who should have been too young to remember.

"I said no, of course."

Of course.

Like that had been the only course of action.

Jessie could have said yes, she supposed. But then she'd be akin to a security blanket—something that was meant to make Erwin feel better. It would have been for his benefit, not hers. And it wasn't Jessie's job to help Erwin come to terms with how his life had turned out.

"I know how he feels, though," she mused. "Wondering how things might have been, if we had been able to agree on a business that we could run together. What it would have been like to have a lifelong companion, rather than spending our evenings alone. Never going on vacation, because what fun is that if you don't have someone to share it with?" Jessie shook her head. "I have to go." And she hurried out, the recipe still clutched in Adeline's hand.

Addie had been wrong.

Jessie hadn't earned it. And she didn't deserve it.

But the next morning, a plaid card sat on Jessie's front porch, same as the other days.

No recipe. It was worse.

The challenge was still on.

And Adeline was upping the ante.

11

Erwin glanced at his phone as it rang. And rang. And rang. It paused, then began ringing once again. It had been doing that for the past three days.

He supposed he couldn't avoid the lawyer forever. But Jessie's refusal—it had changed things.

It shouldn't have. He'd known it was a crazy idea. He'd known she wouldn't say yes. Why would she?

Erwin had hoped a sincere apology would help soften things, as least to the point that they could be on somewhat friendly terms. That would have at least given him something to work with.

But then he'd had to go and ruin it all by proposing.

It shouldn't have come as a surprise that things had ended this way. It had been a crazy idea to think he could sell the restaurant and spend what time he had left with Jessie. How it should have been all along.

Patty had told Erwin he still had plenty of good years, that he was in relatively good health and he shouldn't plan his funeral anytime soon.

But Erwin could read between the lines.

He was on a downward slope that would only get steeper.

Erwin climbed the stairs to where he lived above the restaurant. His saxophone sat in the corner, untouched for the past couple of months. The local jazz band hadn't had any shows since tourist season ended, and he hadn't been in the mood to play.

He lifted it and sat on the bed, playing the first song that came to mind.

The first song that he and Jessie had danced to. They'd been fifteen, and awkward. As Erwin played "Love Will Keep Us Together" by Captain & Tennille, longing flooded through him. Two years after that first dance, he'd learned the song on his saxophone to play for Jessie on Valentine's Day. They'd had their first proper kiss.

Erwin couldn't even make it through the entire song before he had to stop.

Jessie and he were meant to be together. Even when they'd professed to not be able to stand each other, they'd never been able to leave each other alone.

But what could he do about it?

He'd tried to reconcile. She'd turned him down.

Erwin had always been the type of person to keep pushing until he achieved what he'd been after. He'd thought it was a gift, until it had pushed Jessie away all those years ago.

And he wasn't going to make the same mistake now.

But where did that leave him? Just hold on to the restaurant until he died, and then leave it to his niece who lived in Omaha? He had no other family left.

The doorbell rang downstairs, and Erwin's gaze snapped up. He never had visitors. Ever.

Erwin placed the saxophone down on the bed and stuck his head out the second-floor window, hoping to catch a glimpse of who it could be.

He'd had teenagers play pranks on him—ringing the doorbell and running. They hadn't been by for a long time, though. Not since their parents gave them a talking to.

Erwin sucked in a breath.

It wasn't teenagers.

It was Jessie.

"We're closed," he called down.

He knew she wasn't there to eat. But he didn't know what else to say. If she felt like she needed to explain further—if she thought she'd hurt his feelings—she could save it. He didn't want to hear it.

"I haven't eaten seafood since you opened your restaurant," she called up.

She'd used to love shrimp and crab. And fish.

And she'd given it all up, just to spite him.

Jessie was the most stubborn woman Erwin had ever met. And she was just as kind and funny and compassionate. And apparently cruel, if her showing up on his doorstep was any indication.

"I don't have anything to say to you," he called down. "I still stand by my opinion on the rotating Thanksgiving dinner."

"I'm here about what you proposed the other night."

Erwin's heart stalled. Just for a moment. "You said no. And now you feel bad. But you don't have to feel guilty because I take it all back. I don't want to marry you."

Jessie glared up at the window. "Why not?"

"You give me indigestion."

"Well, fine, then. Because you give me heart palpitations. And not the good kind."

"Fine." Erwin slammed his window shut, his breathing fast.

What had he done? Jessie had returned, and he'd dismissed her. But for good reason. He was too old to be playing these games. Jessie's compassionate side had come out, and she didn't like how they'd left things. But that didn't change anything. And he couldn't handle any more heartache.

But then he heard a scream.

Erwin rushed down the stairs faster than he had in years and out the back door of the restaurant. His gaze bounced around wildly, Jessie nowhere to be seen.

"Jessie," he called.

A faint moan was the only response he received, and he moved toward the stairs that led down to the beach. There Jessie was, sprawled out at the bottom of them.

Erwin hurried down the stairs.

"Where does it hurt?" he asked, bending over her. She was holding her knee, and he gingerly touched it. Erwin didn't know what that was supposed to do, or what he was looking for, but he'd always noticed Patty doing it whenever someone was injured.

Jessie pushed herself into a seated position, then stood up.

Erwin blinked. "You're not hurt."

"Physically, no."

The woman was insufferable.

"Jessie, you can't do stuff like that. It's mean. And it's crying wolf. Next time you won't be able to count on me rushing down here to help."

"You wouldn't talk to me. What else was I supposed to do?"

Erwin took a step back from Jessie. "A phone call would have sufficed."

"I did call. Three times. You didn't answer."

Oh.

Erwin released a long sigh. "I'm sorry I messed up the equilibrium we had between us, Jessie. Even if things haven't been perfect, we'd found a way to make it work. I had a panicked moment. A late-life crisis, if you will. And I acted before thinking. If you can forgive me, we can go back to how things were."

"You mean, with you avoiding me? And when we do speak, it's only in annoyed tones, with us taking great care to only agree with each other when necessary?" Jessie's lips twitched up, like the thought amused her.

But that did sum up what their relationship had become. A necessary evil, considering both of them refused to move away from Starlight Ridge. So here they were.

"Yes, that sounds about right."

Jessie slumped onto the sand, pulling her legs into her chest. "I've been receiving challenges from Adeline each day. A means to an end. I'd thought I'd lost the challenge, but Adeline insisted I'd met all the requirements, and the challenges have continued to arrive." She held a square card out to him. "This was today's challenge. My fault for confiding in her. I should have known better."

Erwin hesitated, then reached out and took the card.

Talk to Erwin for thirty minutes. Without being mean.

"You're right. You should have known better," Erwin said, handing the card back to her. "Adeline lives for the ridiculous. And she's made you a part of her game."

Jessie was already shaking her head before he'd had the chance to finish. "It's not like that. Not this time. Adeline... She was concerned about me. Said that I spend all my time focused on others, that I never do anything for myself. Each challenge is meant to help me be happy again. To discover myself. And they have. Things like running in the ocean and eating breakfast for dinner.

They've brought back memories of when we were young. And they have made me happy. Made me feel free."

"And now she's back to doing things for her own amusement. Probably hiding in the bushes somewhere, watching."

Jessie's forehead crinkled. "I don't think so. It's more like she feels that if we can patch things up between us—if we can get through a thirty-minute conversation without insults—maybe I could find more peace in my life."

"And what do you get in exchange for completing the challenges?" Erwin asked. It had to be something good to put her fate in the hands of someone like Adeline. He didn't buy that she was doing this for Jessie's own good. The chocolate shop owner always had something up her sleeve.

Pink crept up Jessie's neck. "That's not important. What is, is that we've managed to talk for fifteen minutes without biting each other's heads off. And that's progress. Maybe we aren't meant to be together, but that doesn't mean we can't be friends. And that is something that would make me very happy. We were a good team, back in the day."

After all that had happened, Jessie thought they could just be friends. That was cute. Maybe she really had reverted to teenage Jessie, because that was the only way she'd be naive enough to believe that.

"I'm sorry, Jess, but I can't be friends with you."

Jessie frowned and folded her arms across her chest. "And yet you can marry me? You can't just propose to someone because you're lonely. Or you feel guilty. And then turn around and shun them because they say no."

"Sure I can. People do it all the time."

Jessie threw her arms in the air. "You're impossible. I thought maybe Adeline was onto something. That maybe we could still care for each other, even if it wasn't in the way it had been. But you never cared for anyone but yourself. And your 'world-famous' shrimp."

Jessie did air quotes, but she hadn't needed them, sarcasm dripping from each word. Maybe she didn't think of his shrimp as world famous, but everyone else did. And they were the only ones whose opinions mattered.

"I'm sorry you feel that way."

Jessie threw one last glare at him before getting to her feet and stalking down the beach. Erwin glanced at his watch. Three-thirty already. He hadn't realized it had gotten so late.

Erwin watched Jessie's retreating figure. He counted to thirteen. Then he began walking after her.

It was a good five minutes before she realized he was back there. She paused mid-step, glanced over her shoulder, and released an exasperated sigh. "Why are you following me?"

"I'm not. We simply have the same destination, and I assumed you wouldn't want to walk with me."

Jessie seemed confused, but then her expression cleared. "The town council meeting. I completely forgot."

She hesitated, then tilted her head in a movement that made it seem like she wanted him to join her.

Erwin assumed he'd misinterpreted the motion, but then Jessie said, "Well, come on. It feels creepy having you back there, stalking me."

"I don't stalk." And he resented the insinuation, but regardless, Erwin quickened his steps until he and Jessie were walking side by side.

Something they hadn't done in a very long time.

And despite how it had come about, Erwin could admit that it was nice.

12

J essie entered the community center, where the town
hall meeting would be starting shortly. She glanced
at her phone, checking to see how long the walk had
taken her and Erwin. Eighteen minutes. That combined
with their earlier conversation should be enough to
consider the challenge complete. They hadn't spoken for
most of the walk, but she was still counting it. That was a
nice thing to do, after all, inviting him to accompany her.

Even if she had accused him of stalking.

Erwin took his place at the head of the table, and Jessie
slipped into a chair at the opposite end. Erwin glanced
around at the empty seats. "Where's Bree and Caleb?"

"They're sick," Leanne said. She had her computer in
front of her, typing away. Probably working on her next
screenplay. "Again. Once you have kids, you get every cold
and flu that breezes through town. Or so I'm told."

"And Adeline?" Erwin said.

As if on cue, Adeline hurried through the door. "Present and accounted for. Sorry, I was just giving Eli last-minute instructions before leaving him in charge of the store. I know he can handle it, but I've made a couple of changes since he was last home."

Adeline eyed the distance that Jessie had placed between herself and Erwin, and raised an eyebrow but didn't say anything as she sat down next to Leanne.

"Well, we'll make this meeting short, then," Erwin said. "Where are we with Thanksgiving preparations? It's only three weeks away. I suppose you all are still set on your rotating dinner."

Jessie half-raised her hand. She hated what she was about to do, but she didn't see any other way. "Actually, with so much sickness spreading around town—Patty also came down with the flu this afternoon—I'm questioning whether that's the wisest course of action."

Erwin leaned back in his chair and eyed the others in the room. "You can't argue with logic. The flu has been going around, and the more locations we visit, the more likely we are to come down with it ourselves."

There was a fair bit of grumbling, but the rest of town council had to concede that having Thanksgiving dinner on the boardwalk, outside, would be the best way to protect the health of the town.

"Originally, each family was in charge of the dinner course that would be served in their home or shop, but since we've switched directions on this thing, I'll need a couple of volunteers to orchestrate preparations," Erwin said, his gaze moving around the room. "And it will need to happen quickly. Time is not on our side."

Everyone dropped their gazes, not wanting to make eye contact. Jessie knew from personal experience that whoever volunteered wouldn't truly be in charge. They'd have to answer to Erwin. And no one wanted that.

"I think you should do it," Jessie ventured. She knew it was a risky move, but she held Erwin's gaze as his eyes narrowed. "You were the one who wanted dinner to be on the boardwalk, per tradition. So you should be in charge. That way, it can be according to your liking."

Adeline jumped on it, not allowing Erwin time to protest. "All in favor of Erwin and Jessie being in charge of preparations, say aye."

Jessie's heart dropped. "Now, wait a minute…"

But everyone's hand was already in the air. All except Erwin and herself.

Erwin had been right. As much as Jessie loved Adeline, she wasn't to be trusted.

"HEY, TRAITOR," Jessie said, catching Adeline before she could leave the community center. "You know what has gone on between Erwin and me. Why would you set me up like that?"

Adeline didn't look the least bit offended and instead

laughed. "You do realize that it's exactly the kind of thing you'd have done, right? I mean, when Travis first arrived in town to take over the hardware store, you set him up to be auctioned for a date, then won the bid so you could give the date to Eliza. I mean, talk about setting people up."

That was a fair point.

"But Travis and Eliza didn't have the history that Erwin and I do," Jessie said. "I can't work with that man. Not after everything that's gone on. Erwin is looking back at his life, wanting to make amends, which is great, except it seems that part of making those amends is winning back my affection. I can't plan an event under those circumstances. It's going to be the worst Thanksgiving this town has ever had."

"Or the most interesting," Adeline said, hooking her arm through Jessie's and walking with her as they exited the building. She paused and turned Jessie so they faced each other. "Look, I'm not expecting you to fall back in love with Erwin. I just think it's about time you two at least admit that you stopped hating each other a long time ago. Pretending that you do isn't healthy. And it isn't good for this town."

"I don't hate Erwin. And I've never said I did. Does he drive me bonkers? Yes. Annoy me on purpose? Again, yes. But I don't hate the man."

"Then why do you act like you do? It's like a show you two put on for the town. As if you want there to be no mistake that you do not like Erwin, and vice versa."

"I—" Jessie's words left her. Because she knew there might be some truth to that. "Fine. I'll plan the Thanksgiving dinner. But only because we're behind schedule and have a lot to do in the next couple of weeks. It makes sense to have the two most senior members of town council head things up." Adeline's eyes brightened, so Jessie quickly added, "I wouldn't get your hopes up. We're planning Thanksgiving dinner, not a wedding."

Adeline unhooked her arm from Jessie's and sauntered away toward home. "We'll see about that," she called over her shoulder.

A sinking feeling settled in Jessie's stomach. She had always enjoyed a bit of small-town intervention, when it had been her doing the intervening.

Now, it terrified her.

THE PHONE RANG seven times before Erwin answered. Not that Jessie was counting. She'd begun to wonder if Erwin even had an answering machine.

"Hello?"

That voice.

Jessie had heard it plenty over the years. But not over the phone. And never on purpose.

"Jess?"

She cleared her throat. "Erwin, we need to get things rolling for Thanksgiving. You got your wish, and now we need to move quickly. I've made a list dividing the tasks between us and—"

"Great. I'll be right over so we can discuss it. See you in thirty minutes."

And the line went dead.

She stared at the phone in her hand. That was not what Jessie had been expecting—or wanting.

How had that even happened?

She went over the conversation in her head, wondering if it had been something she'd said. Or her tone. Had she subconsciously insinuated that she wanted Erwin to come over?

No. After going over the conversation carefully, she could decisively say that the miscommunication had not been on her end.

And then the panic set in.

Erwin was coming over.

It shouldn't have mattered. It was only Erwin.

But he'd never been inside this house before. Passed by the front, yes. But never inside.

First things first.

Jessie rushed into the bathroom to check her reflection. Her hair was out of control. Nothing a brush couldn't fix. She'd need a little bit of make-up. Nothing to impress, of course, but he couldn't go around thinking she didn't take care of herself. Or that those bags under her eyes were normally there.

A different top might be nice too. Something that was casual but didn't imply that Jessie stayed in her pajamas all day.

Which she didn't.

Usually.

Jessie glanced at her watch. Seven minutes left.

Just enough time to straighten up the coffee table, fluff up the throw pillows, and light a candle. Not a romantic one, mind. Just one that would give her home the scent of apple spice. It was fall, after all, and 'twas the season.

Exactly thirty minutes from when Jessie had realized Erwin was coming over, there was a knock on her door.

She straightened her blouse, smoothed her hair, then opened the door.

There were no flowers this time, thank goodness. Because this wasn't a date. This was a planning session. And flowers would have been inappropriate, especially after the words they'd exchanged at dinner.

The flowers.

They were still sitting in a vase on the countertop.

He'd know that she'd kept them. And that she'd liked them.

There was nothing she could do about it now, though, short of slamming the door in Erwin's face so she could dump them. And she didn't think that would go over very well.

Maybe he wouldn't notice.

"Good morning, Erwin," Jessie said, though not opening the door any wider. "You really didn't need to come all this way. We could have discussed things over the phone."

"I'm able to bounce my ideas off someone better if we meet in person," Erwin said. "And it sounds like you have a lot of ideas."

Jessie was able to read between the lines. Erwin didn't want Jessie taking over things, so he was here to make sure his voice was heard.

Erwin produced something from behind his back, and Jessie's heart stalled.

But they weren't flowers.

Again, no disappointment. Mostly.

It was a large cloth bag, but what might be in it, Jessie couldn't tell.

"What's a good planning session without food? I brought brunch from the diner. Quiche and orange juice."

Jessie could smell the quiche. Despite her having already eaten breakfast, her stomach grumbled. She loved the diner's quiche. This wasn't a date, she reminded herself as she opened the door wider, gesturing for Erwin to come in. Yes, it was only the two of them. And he'd brought food.

"Oh, the flowers I gave you look nice in that vase, don't they?" Erwin asked as he placed the food on the counter.

Jessie forced a smile and begged her heart rate to slow. So what, he'd noticed the vase. That meant Erwin now felt appreciated and would be more likely to go along with her ideas for the town's Thanksgiving feast.

"Yes, they were too pretty not to put out for display," she said.

Erwin folded the now-empty bag and placed it next to the food. With the task complete, his attention moved to the rest of the house. "I like what you've done here. It suits you."

"Thank you." Jessie didn't know what else to say to that. Erwin had given her what sounded like a genuine compliment. There was no bitterness underlying his words. Usually when the two of them spoke, it was through pointed jabs and sarcasm. And if a kind word was spoken, it was usually quickly followed up by one of the two. Jessie was unsure how to handle this new dynamic.

"Plates," she said, hurrying into the kitchen. "We'll need plates and glasses and forks."

"And napkins," Erwin added.

Okay. Things were going well. The conversation had devolved into listing items needed for a meal, but at least they were talking.

"I'm looking forward to seeing your list of actionable items," Erwin said as he divided the quiche onto the two plates. "Because I brought one of my own, as well."

Jessie paused. "We already have one. What good is two?"

"You're right, I suppose," Erwin said, lifting a shoulder. "We could just use mine. But I wouldn't mind seeing yours." He smiled then stuffed a large bite of quiche into his mouth.

Jessie's jaw clenched.

Scratch that. Things were not going well.

And it was about to get worse.

13

E rwin could tell Jessie wasn't pleased that he'd made his own list of ideas for the Thanksgiving dinner. But what had she expected? She might have missed any number of things, and he needed to make sure they were thorough and this thing went off without a hitch. It had been Erwin who had insisted they couldn't do away with tradition, and he didn't want to be proved wrong.

"What, I'm not allowed to have ideas now?" he asked, taking his food to the coffee table and settling in on the couch. "We're supposed to be a team."

"Yes," Jessie said, bringing her own food over. "In execution. But I've always been the better planner."

Erwin frowned. "What makes you say that? I think I've done pretty well for myself. Couldn't have the success I do without attention to details."

Jessie was quiet for a moment as she took a bite of the

quiche. Her eyes lit up momentarily, as if she was savoring the bite, but then they clouded again when they turned to him.

That was one of the things Erwin missed most about Jessie. The way her eyes would light up when she saw him. How carefree her laugh was, and the way it could brighten any room. He didn't remember the last time he'd been able to make her laugh. Of course, it had been a long time since he'd tried.

"The problem is that you are so focused on the details that you miss the forest for the trees," she said. "The purpose of the event is for people to have fun. Enjoy each other's company. And, of course, eat good food."

"What makes you think people won't have fun with my plan? They always have fun. Every year, I get compliments on how much people enjoy the event."

Jessie hesitated, and he could tell there was something she wanted to say but was unsure if she should.

"What?" he asked.

"They do have fun," she said slowly, "but haven't you asked yourself why they wanted to switch it up this year? Why they wanted to do the rotating dinner?"

No, Erwin hadn't. He'd assumed it was because they'd momentarily lost their minds, and then left it at that.

Jessie could tell he hadn't even considered it, and she shook her head. "Our Thanksgiving feast is the same every year. The same food. The same speeches. People even sit in the same places, almost like we've been doing it so long, they now have reserved seats."

"Routine is comforting," Erwin said.

"To a point. But they wanted to switch it up this year. Try something different."

Erwin snorted. "They only think they want something different."

"They voted," Jessie said with an exasperated sigh. She set her fork down. "Erwin, things change. They're meant to. And I'm sorry, but you can't stop it."

Erwin thought back to the restaurant. It wasn't that he was against change—he'd been seriously considering selling Seaside Bay and moving somewhere new. Trying something different. But he'd also realized over the past week that he wasn't meant for it. Even though he no longer needed to be at the restaurant full-time, he enjoyed checking in each day at the same time with the same people. He enjoyed taking Donna for a walk at the same time in the same places and greeting the same people as he did so. It was comforting.

Switching up Thanksgiving dinner, it was unnecessary. Uncomfortable.

"Of course I can stop change," Erwin said, taking out the piece of paper he'd typed his plan on. He smoothed it out on the coffee table in front of him. "I'm head of town council."

Jessie snorted and leaned back in her seat. "You're on town council and happen to lead the vote, but you don't get more of a vote than the rest of us." Her lips dipped, and she suddenly looked sad. "What happened, Ernie? You used to be so...light. Excited about life. Fun."

Erwin bristled at the nickname. "I'm still fun. I play my saxophone with the town band. And I was the lead in the Christmas play last year."

"You were Scrooge in *A Christmas Carol*, but still, that's a fair point. Of course, the play was scripted. When was the last time you had spontaneous fun?"

That was an absurd question. Whoever found spontaneity fun? It was chaotic. And terrifying. How was a person supposed to plan for what came next?

Erwin's relationship with Jessie had been nothing but spontaneous for the many years they'd spent together. No plan.

And look how that had turned out.

When Erwin didn't answer, Jessie gave a nod, like she'd expected as much.

"I have a set of challenges for you," she said. "You do one every day for the next week, and we'll go with your plan for Thanksgiving dinner. You don't, we do my plan."

Jessie was sounding a lot like Adeline in that moment, and he didn't like it. "I don't even know what your plan is."

"And you won't. Unless you lose, of course. Then you'll learn every detail." Jessie smiled, like she couldn't wait.

The thought of Jessie in complete control of the event terrified Erwin. "I don't see why I have to do anything to earn the right to have my ideas listened to."

Jessie stopped at that and seemed to actually think it over. "You're right. Everyone deserves to have their voice heard. But that's the thing. Everyone on council made their voice heard, and you still insisted that yours was the correct one."

That wasn't fair. Erwin may have strong opinions, but he knew others had something to contribute.

"All right. I wouldn't want to be accused of taking over. We'll look at both of our ideas and come to a mutual agreement. Like the mature adults that we are."

"Great," Jessie said. "Now, I know that the giant inflatable turkey is one of our traditions—"

Erwin stopped her right there. "You know Teddy is my favorite part of Thanksgiving." And that just proved that he was fun, because only a fun person would choose a fifteen-foot turkey as their favorite thing about their town's festivities.

"I know," Jessie said. "Mine too. But he's looking a bit worse for wear. I was thinking we could get a new Thanksgiving mascot. I doubt we could find one that is exactly like Teddy, but he, or she, would be similar enough that I don't think people would mind."

And there Jessie went, trying to change the one thing that Erwin had thought untouchable.

"Never mind, I'll take your little challenge. But it has to start today, because Thanksgiving is going to be a disaster if we waste any more time."

Jessie frowned at his response, but then nodded. "All right. First challenge. Tell me a joke."

Erwin stared. That was it? The challenges Adeline had been giving Jessie had her doing things like running through the freezing-cold ocean. He'd expected the same treatment, considering it was where Jessie had gotten the idea in the first place.

"A joke?" he asked.

Jessie nodded, a slight smile appearing on her lips.

Erwin enjoyed a good joke as much as the next person, but he rarely remembered them. He'd laugh and then someone else would tell a joke, and the first one would already be forgotten.

"A joke. Sure. I thought you said you were giving me a challenge," he said, smiling, as if this was the easiest thing in the world. "A joke..."

Jessie was still smiling, but it seemed to have morphed into something else. Concern, maybe? She was worried that he couldn't handle even the simplest of challenges.

"Okay, I got it," Erwin said. He couldn't remember any jokes, so he'd just have to make one up himself.

Jessie brightened, like she couldn't wait to see what he'd come up with. He hoped he wouldn't let her down. Not that he cared what she thought of him. But no one liked to have a joke fall flat, receiving nothing but uncomfortable silence on the other end of the punchline.

"Okay, a pregnant woman walks into a bar." He paused for dramatic effect. "BOING!"

He smiled, pleased with himself for being able to come up with something in the moment.

But Jessie didn't even give him a courtesy laugh. Instead, she looked perplexed.

"You know, because it was a metal bar," he said, stumbling over his words. "And she's pregnant, so when her stomach hit it, she bounced off."

Jessie was still staring, but the confusion had cleared, and then a giant laugh burst from her. "I had understood it, but I've just never heard a joke like it." Her laughter intensified, and it filled Erwin with a sense of pride. He'd created a joke himself, and it had made Jessie laugh. That was all he could have asked for.

"I'm glad you thought it was a good one. Challenge complete, then, I suppose?"

Jessie was now laughing so hard, tears were streaming down her cheeks. He'd thought the joke was amusing, but not funny enough for the woman to be crying.

"It was terrible, Ernie," she said, gasping for breath. "But the fact that it was so bad brought it full circle to funny again."

Oh. Well, she did say it was funny, so he'd take it.

"Great." He clapped his hands together. "What's the next challenge?"

Jessie wagged a finger, still trying to pull herself together. "Nope. One a day, remember?"

Erwin tried not to show his disappointment, even

though he'd wanted nothing more than to finish the challenge as quickly as possible.

Maybe Jessie was right. Maybe he'd forgotten how to have fun.

But then he glanced at his plan for the Thanksgiving feast.

No, he knew how to have fun. And he was going to prove it by winning this challenge and doing this event the right way.

14

J essie glanced at her own challenge card from that
morning. Only sixteen days to go.

*Pay it forward. Challenge someone else for at least
seven of your remaining days.*

She'd thought it was a silly challenge. Paying it forward
usually had to do with serving someone else. Anony-
mously paying for their morning coffee. Raking leaves
when they weren't home. Stuff like that.

But what did challenging them contribute?

Jessie didn't have to think on it, because one word
immediately sprang to mind.

Joy.

Adeline's mission had been to help Jessie rediscover
childlike wonder. Joy. And she was asking Jessie to do the
same for someone else.

Jessie hadn't known who she might choose. Originally,

she'd thought maybe Patty would enjoy something like that. Patty had been working as the doctor for their small town for as long as she'd had her medical license, and even a little before. She spent her days and nights tending to others, never complaining.

She would be a good choice, but Jessie had changed her mind when Erwin had shown up on her doorstep. A shadow of the man she'd once been engaged to. He had been full of life at one point, and that joke he'd come up with—that had been exactly the type of thing the younger version of him would have created. Corny, of course. But he'd find it so funny himself that everyone else couldn't help but laugh along.

Jessie hadn't been able to laugh at first, taken aback by the joke. Not because it wasn't funny, but because it was so Erwin.

She hadn't expected that.

Jessie also hadn't expected the sudden attraction she'd felt for the man. And all because of one ridiculous joke.

She shook the thoughts from her head. Erwin wasn't the only one in need of childlike wonder, and Adeline had never said Jessie couldn't challenge more than one person.

This was fun. Addictive. And she needed more.

So Jessie slipped on her jacket and hurried out into the crisp air. She knew Patty would be at the office—she always was—and Jessie smiled to herself as she patted the pocket where she'd slipped the challenge card.

She had considered regifting the cards that Adeline

had given her, but each person in this town was unique and deserved their own personal challenge.

And who knew everyone better than Jessie? No one, that was who.

Erwin had needed that joke, just like Patty needed to dance like no one was watching, as cliché as that was.

Something small. Something fun. And something that would bring joy.

The more Jessie thought of what challenges she could do for others, the more excited she got about doing the activities herself, no challenge needed. She was certain she'd be dancing to "Footloose" in her kitchen before the day was through. Not because someone had challenged her, but because it sounded fun.

And Jessie needed all the fun she could get.

Everyone could.

Jessie rounded a corner, the clinic coming into view. Someone was just entering. Looked like Leanne.

Perfect.

She waited at the side of the building for another ten minutes, enough time for Leanne to do any necessary paperwork, and then Jessie peeked her head in. The receptionist, Sandy, had her back turned, filing something. The rest of the waiting room was empty.

Careful to ease the door closed behind her, Jessie crept forward and gently placed the challenge card on the counter. She realized too late that she'd forgotten to write Patty's name on the front.

Sandy, however, was already finishing up and turning back to the reception desk. Too late now.

Jessie spun around to leave but was called back.

"Jessie, can I help you with something?"

She slowly turned. "You know, I meant to go to the scuba shop and somehow ended up here instead. My mind isn't what it used to be." She raised a finger. "But it's the darnedest thing. I noticed a card for Patty on the desk there."

Sandy raised a skeptical eyebrow. "How do you know? There's no name."

"But this is her clinic, isn't it? It just stands to reason that it would be for her."

"You thought this was the scuba shop—even though it's three streets over on the boardwalk," Sandy said, her words slow. "And then you noticed a suspicious-looking card with no name on it, and you believe it belongs to Patty."

Jessie raised a shoulder. "That sounds about right. Of course, what you do with the card is up to you. It could be for anyone, I suppose. Even your next patient. But logic says that it's more likely..."

The door to the clinic opened. And in walked Erwin.

Of course.

"Erwin," Sandy said. "Right on time, as usual."

When Erwin saw Jessie, he paused, confusion crossing his face, but he quickly recovered and hurried over to the desk to sign in.

Sandy eyed Jessie, a twinkle in her eye, and as Erwin straightened, she said, "Someone left a card for you. Anonymous."

Jessie felt heat rush into her cheeks. She knew Sandy was messing with her—seeing what Jessie would do. But if the receptionist expected Jessie to panic and snatch back the "anonymous" card, she was about to be disappointed.

That being said, Jessie needed to get out of there before Erwin opened that envelope. He'd know it was from her. But he'd have no idea that it hadn't been intended for him.

"Well, good to see you, as always," Jessie said, waving to Sandy and hurrying out, her footsteps quick.

She didn't manage to get further than the sidewalk before Erwin burst through the front door. "Beyoncé?"

Jessie plastered on a smile and turned slowly. "I like her music."

"Should I read too much into the fact that she sang, 'If you liked it then you should have put a ring on it?' Or did you have a different song in mind?"

Jessie stilled, but then her lips quirked up at the edges. "How on earth do you know that song?" Honestly, it was a miracle that either of them even knew who Beyoncé was, let alone her song lyrics.

Erwin looked embarrassed at the admission and raised a shoulder. "One of my waitresses was obsessed with the song. Would play it over and over in the kitchen."

Jessie took a step forward. "But you knew who sang it." She allowed herself a full smile. "You like the song."

A blush crept up Erwin's otherwise very white neck. "It's catchy, that's all."

Jessie couldn't trap the giggle that escaped. She sounded like a twelve-year-old girl, but that was no different from the image that had immediately popped into her mind of Erwin shaking his hips and singing into a spatula.

Erwin's embarrassment turned to annoyance. "You said one challenge a day. I'm not doing it."

"Fine," Jessie said, waving a hand in the air like she didn't care. "Give it to Patty, then. She won't know the difference."

"I will," Erwin said.

"Good."

Erwin frowned before stalking back into the medical clinic.

Jessie didn't worry about what happened to the challenge card. There were plenty more where that came from, and she'd work on a better distribution system to ensure it made it into the right hands the next time.

15

If anyone other than Jessie discovered what was on the video file Erwin had just sent her, he'd have to move from Starlight Ridge. No, he'd have to fake his own death. Then move.

And he'd just sent it to the biggest gossip the town had.

As soon as Erwin had pressed send, he'd regretted it. He'd begged the teenager who'd helped him upload the file to get the email back. To cancel it. And then delete the video file from his computer forever.

You'd think that teenagers, with all the technological know-how they bragged about, would be able to fulfill this simple request.

But no. He'd informed Erwin that there was no way to get that file back. That he could delete it from his computer, but the recipient would still have the video.

Erwin couldn't believe he'd been so stupid. Wanted to

prove something to Jessie, though he now couldn't imagine it had been important enough to send that video.

And he certainly wouldn't tell Jessie that he'd recorded the video months earlier, and not as a dare. He'd done it for his brother's daughter. Erwin hadn't seen her in years, but ever since his brother's death, he'd tried to keep in touch with the family. There were limited ways he knew how to stay connected, and this had been one that his niece had fully appreciated.

He'd had to pay a teenager to help him send the video that time too.

"Donna, I need a walk," he said as soon as the teenage boy had left with twenty dollars crumpled in his fist. Erwin reached down and petted his golden retriever on the head. She nuzzled his hand, and he squatted, rubbing his cheek on her soft fur. She rewarded him with a sloppy kiss, and Erwin laughed. He pulled a leash from under the kitchen table, one of the many locations where a leash had been haphazardly tossed to the side.

"You know I'm fun," he said to Donna as they embarked on their nighttime journey. "That's what counts." The sun had already set, and the stars were just coming out. Millions of them blinked from their places in the sky, and Erwin breathed in the cool air.

No, he could never leave Starlight Ridge. Even if the entire town saw that video—which they would—this was home. It was the same reason that he and Jessie had tolerated each other's company for so many years.

Jessie.

She'd thought he'd proposed—the most recent time—because he was scared to die alone. Turned him down without even having to think about it.

He couldn't blame her, considering their history and the abruptness of it all. And it was true, he was scared. He'd been having check-ups at the clinic more frequently, just to make sure Patty didn't miss anything that might pop up. Never knew with the body. It could be your best friend one minute, then turn on you the next.

Patty had given him the same news today that he'd received at his past three appointments. He was fine. A little dusty. A little worse for wear. But he was fine.

And apparently dancing to Beyoncé.

He'd bet that Jessie would have enjoyed coming up with the choreography with him for the video. Seemed like the kind of thing she'd enjoy. And dancing it—she would have been the star of the show.

He released a long breath.

If only.

He'd thought those words a lot over the years.

If only he and Jessie had been able to figure things out.

If only they hadn't broken up.

If only people could see him for who he really was, rather than the broken version they'd become accustomed to.

If only he hadn't sent that video, which would do just that—show Starlight Ridge who Erwin Anderson really was. A crazy old man. This was something they'd likely suspected for a long time but could never prove.

Erwin had been so lost in his thoughts, he'd allowed Donna to lead him where she wished. And by the time he realized where they were, they'd ended up at Jessie's spot on the beach. No one else had a place designated just for them. But when Adeline's husband, Eli, had discovered that Jessie had sat in the same spot for every sunset stroll since she was a young girl, he'd erected a fence around it, complete with a sign.

Donna barked, and Erwin released her leash, thinking she wanted to go for a run. But instead, she leaped forward, a shriek following soon after. And then a laugh.

Jessie had been sitting in her spot, in the dark.

"What are you doing out here by yourself?" Erwin asked, attempting to pull Donna back. "The sun is long gone, not to mention the rest of the town."

"Enjoying the quiet," she said.

Erwin's gaze landed on the ocean. The moon's reflection could be seen in it, as well as the stars. "Yes, I can understand that." He clipped Donna's leash back onto her collar. "I'm sorry to ruin it for you. We'll get out of your hair."

"You weren't here for the sunset stroll," Jessie said. It caught him off guard. She'd noticed his absence.

Erwin nodded, though he then realized she likely couldn't see the movement. "I got distracted."

Jessie chuckled softly. "Did it, by any chance, have something to do with Beyoncé?"

He was grateful she couldn't see how red his face must be at that moment. "She *is* quite distracting."

Jessie laughed, but then grew quiet again. "You don't have to do that challenge. I'll come up with something else."

That was when Erwin realized she hadn't seen the video. She'd been here for the sunset stroll and never left. Which meant he still had a chance to make sure no one in town would ever see it.

He couldn't very well alert her to its existence, though, or else she'd look at it first chance she got.

"It's getting cold, Jess. Why don't I walk you home?"

Her head whipped toward him, like she was surprised by the offer. And he could understand why. But he had to get to her computer.

What he'd do with it when he got there was a problem he'd deal with later.

First step, get into Jessie's house.

The thought sent a thrill through him, making him feel like a regular James Bond. He'd never have considered doing something like this last year, let alone last month. Jessie had been a bad influence on him as of late. Or good, depending on how you looked at it.

Jessie moved to stand. "All right." She seemed to be having trouble getting up, and Erwin held out his arm to help her. "Thank you."

She held on tight as she pulled herself from the chair. They hadn't stood this close in a very long time, and Erwin's brain began to get hazy. Even now, after all these years, Jessie's hair still smelled like the ocean. It had always intoxicated him, how she could be so much a part of the place she lived—a place she loved.

After arriving on her feet, Jessie still clung on to him, like she was afraid to let go.

"You got your land legs back?" he asked, his voice gruff. He hadn't meant for it to come out like that, but it seemed he was having as much trouble speaking as he was thinking.

Jessie took a step back. "I believe so. It seems I sat too long, and my limbs forgot what they were meant for. Thank you for your assistance."

Erwin grunted in response, afraid he'd give away what Jessie's presence was doing to him. This was why he preferred to avoid her. Because, even now, she could always do him in.

And she'd made it very clear where she stood on the issue of her and Erwin.

The two of them walked in silence. Erwin tried to speak several times, but nothing ever came out. He didn't know what to say.

When Donna abruptly pulled forward, trying to get him to walk faster, Erwin tripped, and Jessie rested a hand on his arm, steadying him.

"Hold on there, girl. We'll get there soon enough," she

said. In the dark, Erwin could almost imagine they were on one of the many walks they'd enjoyed when they were younger.

But then a thought struck him.

Donna.

Jessie would never invite Erwin inside with the dog, nor would he want her to. Donna was a wonderful dog, but not always the best behaved. Jessie's home would be covered in sand and broken glass by the time they left.

They moved away from the beach and onto the small road that passed in front of Jessie's home.

"Thank you for the company," Jessie said. "I think I can take it from here."

Normally Erwin would agree.

But what about the video?

It would raise eyebrows if Erwin invited himself in, and what was he going to do, tie up Donna outside?

It was time he admitted defeat. By the time he awoke the next morning, all of Starlight Ridge would have seen the video, and there was nothing he could do about it.

Erwin was about to say goodnight when Jessie added, "Unless you and Donna are thirsty. You could come inside for a drink before heading back. If you want. No obligation." She paused, seeming flustered.

This was his chance.

But it suddenly felt wrong. It would be going in under false pretenses. Her kindness would be shadowed by deceit.

How did James Bond do it all the time? Was he ever at war with himself, or had he been doing it so long that it now came easy?

"I'm afraid Donna isn't a very good houseguest," Erwin said. "Thank you for the offer, though. Next time."

Jessie waved a hand in the air. "Nothing that a good bowl of water won't fix."

There were actually a lot of Donna's behaviors that hydration didn't fix. But Jessie didn't seem to be interested in hearing them because she'd already spun toward home.

"Come on, Donna," she called. "Let's show Ernie what a good girl you are."

Since when did Jessie like dogs? Specifically, since when did she like Donna?

Donna bounded forward, and Erwin let go of her leash to avoid being pulled after her.

Oh, boy. This wasn't going to end well.

16

J essie unlocked the front door, and a giant mass of fur
ran past her, bounding into the house. "Donna, it's
not polite to run indoors," she called.

It may have been a mistake inviting them both in. For
one, Jessie didn't know anything about owning a dog.
Didn't even like them, most of the time. And two, after
thirty years of Erwin never visiting her home, this was the
second time in one day that she'd invited him inside.

Some would call that progress.

It was terrifying, was what it was. Boundaries were
being blurred.

"Donna, sit," Erwin said in a sharp, no-nonsense voice.

The dog immediately jumped from the couch and sat
back on her haunches. Jessie was impressed.

"Would you like water or tea?" she asked, moving to
the kitchen cupboards. A large mixing bowl should work

for Donna's water dish. As for her and Erwin, Jessie looked for something that was a step up from paper cups but a step down from champagne glasses.

After a moment of deliberation, Jessie reached for a mug that had a cartoon chicken on it. It had curly hair and glasses and looked exhausted, like it had just woken up. The chicken wore a bathrobe, had bags under its eyes, and held an exact replica of the mug its image was on.

Yup, this was perfect.

"Water is fine," he said.

Jessie placed ice in her mug—it had a beaver who looked remarkably like Erwin's chicken—and then filled both with water from the fridge.

"You remembered no ice," he said when Jessie handed him the mug.

"Hard to forget, considering every Thanksgiving dinner at the boardwalk, you insist we have one water pitcher on each table with ice, and one without. No one ever drinks out of the one without ice, so you essentially get five water pitchers to yourself."

The words came out harsher than Jessie had intended, and she wished she could try again. She hadn't invited Erwin inside just so they could fight.

But to her surprise, Erwin nodded, as if he was agreeing with her.

"I suppose that is a little excessive, isn't it? I'll fix that this year."

Jessie blinked rapidly, words escaping her. "Okay. Good. Sounds like a plan."

Erwin shifted in his seat, then glanced at his watch, looking anxious to leave. But when he stood, he didn't excuse himself and Donna. Instead, he asked if he could borrow Jessie's computer.

She hadn't realized he even knew how to use one. It wasn't that she had bought into the stereotype that older people didn't know how to use technology. It was just that Erwin had always been against it. He did have a computer for business purposes, but she'd always assumed it was meant for his employees to use. As far as she knew, the extent of Erwin's knowledge had been applied to an old digital video recorder he'd purchased so he could record town events for the Starlight Ridge historical society.

"Um...sure. Is everything okay?"

Erwin hesitated. "It will be soon."

That was ominous.

Jessie directed him to the guest bedroom on the left, which doubled as an office. She'd never actually had houseguests, but if she did, she'd be ready.

When Erwin disappeared into the office, Donna ran to the mixing bowl and began lapping up the water with such furor, half of the water ended up on the floor around the bowl.

"Oh, come now. Where are your manners?" Jessie asked.

The sounds of cursing caught Jessie by surprise, and

her gaze landed on the office. Erwin wasn't one to swear, but technology did seem to have that effect on him.

"I better go help him," she told Donna, patting her on the head. "You have this cleaned up by the time I get back, okay?"

Jessie hurried into the office, and she wasn't certain what to make of the scene in front of her.

Erwin was hunched over the keyboard, seemingly punching every key on it as he repeated, "Delete. Delete. Come on, why won't you go away? And...delete."

He growled in frustration.

"Maybe I can help," Jessie said, approaching him from behind.

Erwin froze, his body blocking the computer screen. "It's okay. I think I got it." A pause. "Yup, there it goes. All taken care of."

Liar.

"What is so important that it couldn't wait until you got home?" Jessie asked, pushing past him. And that was when she saw it.

A video of Erwin dancing. She reached over Erwin to unmute it, and "All the Single Ladies" burst through the speakers. Except, he wasn't just dancing. It was choreographed.

Her eyes widened. She hadn't seen this side of Erwin, ever. Even when they'd been dating. He'd had a fun side, sure. But he'd always claimed to not be a dancer.

"You cannot tell anyone about this," Erwin said, his

tone panicked. His breaths were coming fast, and he looked like he was going to hyperventilate. "I should never have sent it. I thought I could delete it before you saw it, but every time I clicked on something, it just made the image larger or..."

And then Jessie did the unthinkable.

She kissed Erwin.

In one fluid movement, she closed the distance between them and placed her lips on his, her hands resting on each side of his head.

Jessie stumbled backwards. Because she did not know where that had come from. There had been something about that video. The way it had brought memories of a better time flooding back. The way Erwin was smiling as he danced. It was a goofy smile, like he was embarrassed, but she could also tell that he was happy.

That had been the Erwin Jessie had fallen in love with.

The one she missed.

And the one she'd thought was gone forever.

"I'm sorry," Jessie said, wiping her lips with the back of her hand. "I don't...have an explanation."

Erwin blinked fast, and it seemed like he might be in shock. His gaze finally met hers. "This is what does it for you? Men who dance to Beyoncé?"

"No, just when you do," she said. There she went again, saying things she shouldn't. Why was she so impulsive?

Jessie glanced at her watch, and she understood. Nine

o'clock. It was past her bedtime. She was always impulsive when she was tired.

Apparently, Erwin was too, because the next moment, his lips were back on hers. And they were hungry.

It took a second for it to register, but then Jessie wrapped her hands around the back of his neck and pulled him in tighter.

Erwin lost his balance and stumbled backwards and into the office chair. Jessie followed him. She straddled his lap, leaning in, her hair creating a curtain around his face. Her breath hitched when his hands slipped under the back of her shirt.

Their passionate kisses didn't last long—they didn't have the stamina they used to—but when they finally broke apart, Jessie realized she'd been keeping Erwin at arm's length for the past thirty years because she'd been afraid of this moment.

Afraid to realize she still had feelings for her ex-fiancé.

Afraid of forgiving him.

Afraid of making him a part of her life again.

It had been him who had wronged her. She was sure of that.

But none of that mattered now. Not with her still sitting on his lap. Not with him wrapping a lock of her hair around his finger, then watching it fall.

"I..." Jessie scooted off Erwin's lap and straightened her blouse. "I think it's about time I turned in for the night."

Erwin cleared his throat, stood, and gave a curt nod. He

was all business, the glimpse of his former self now all but gone. "Yes, I've kept Donna out too long." He moved to leave the room but paused and turned. "Why did you kiss me?"

Oh, they were doing this, were they?

Jessie didn't want to talk about it. Didn't want to think about it. At least until after Erwin had left.

Then she wouldn't be able to stop herself from going over every detail. About the way his lips had fit perfectly with hers—as if no time had passed. About the way he'd held her like he never wanted to let go.

The way he used to.

"It has been a long time for me, Erwin. Haven't been alone with a man for years. Guess the moment got to me."

Erwin's lips dipped in disappointment, and Jessie hated herself for saying what she had. She knew it wasn't true. That kiss hadn't been out of desperation. It hadn't been because he was the only available man she might have a chance with.

He gave a small nod—one that said he'd thought as much but had been hoping for a different answer.

It broke Jessie's heart.

"That video made me realize you aren't gone," she blurted out. "That the Erwin I fell in love with never left. And I haven't wanted to see it. I've wanted to see you as the villain in my life's story."

Erwin's gaze met Jessie's. His face was weathered, his movements slower, but he was still Ernie.

"All I ever wanted was to make you happy," he said, his words slow. "But I failed. And you had every right to leave. You deserved to live your own dream, not someone else's. I'm sorry I couldn't give you that."

Jessie's breath hitched. Erwin had taken responsibility for what had happened between them, but she hadn't.

"I'm sorry for the hurtful things I said." Jessie's voice caught. "They weren't fair. Or true."

There. It was out in the open.

Erwin stepped in close. "If only we'd done this thirty years ago."

"Let's just think about tonight," Jessie said, her voice soft.

Erwin pulled his fingers through her hair, and she leaned into his hand. "All right." His lips found hers once again. But these kisses were softer. More thoughtful. Like he was savoring every one.

And Jessie continued to savor them, long after he was gone.

17

E rwin slept in the next day. He didn't remember the last time he hadn't been up before Donna. But there she was, standing over him, her face inches from his, staring.

"Morning," he grumbled.

His head pounded, and he reached over to grab his water glass from the nightstand.

Water.

Jessie.

Memories of the previous evening flooded over him. The same memories that had kept him awake well into the night.

The memories had been accompanied by confusion. Fear. And excitement.

But what to do with it all?

Donna pawed at the bed. She wanted to go outside to relieve herself.

"Okay, okay. I'm getting up."

Erwin forced himself into a seated position. It was cold, and he was tempted to climb back under the covers. That proved he definitely wasn't himself today.

It took three tries and two cups of coffee, but Erwin finally made it outside with Donna.

He hadn't made it very far up the beach when he heard a woman call his name from behind. He turned and squinted, compensating for his worsening eyesight, but could only see a small shape bouncing up and down in the distance.

"Wait up," she called.

The sounds of feet hitting the sand.

Adeline came into focus not long after. "Wow, you keep a good pace," she said, bending over and panting.

"You okay?" he asked, freeing Donna from her leash so she could run to greet their friend. Which she promptly did by jumping on Adeline and nearly knocking her over.

"Hang on there," she said with a laugh, and wrapped her arms around the big dog. "I tried calling you at the restaurant, and when you didn't answer, I got worried."

Erwin raised an eyebrow. Him going out wasn't so unusual. In fact, he should have been outside an hour earlier. "Why?"

"Well, you know, because of everything going on with Jessie. I know it's my fault—that I'm the one who instigated

it. I didn't mean to, of course. Didn't know that I had inadvertently forced Jessie into a date with you. But then what
happened next... I just really thought that if you two spent
some time together—you know, not fighting—that you
might be able to give things another go. But then I
heard—"

Erwin held up a hand to stop Adeline, annoyance
bubbling in his chest. He was still trying to sort out his
feelings with Jessie, and she'd already blabbed about it to
everyone. These types of things were meant to be private.

"Addie, this is something that Jessie and I need to work
out ourselves. I thought she had enough decency to at least
come to me before talking with everyone she knew, but I
should have known better. This is Jessie, after all. Give us
at least a few days to figure out if the kiss even meant
anything, and then we can talk again, okay?"

Adeline stared. And blinked. "Sorry?"

Oh. The longer Addie stared, the more Erwin realized
there was a possibility he'd misread the situation.

"Um...Adeline. I interrupted and didn't allow you to
finish, which was quite rude of me. What had you been
going to say?"

Adeline blinked a couple of times, like she was
attempting to bring herself back to the present. "Just that
Patty had mentioned you've been going to the clinic a lot
lately, and I wondered if the stress of Jessie's challenges
and everything...if that had been a bit much. I know that I
tend to cross the line, and honestly don't even see the line

until after I've passed it. And then you didn't answer your phone, and I worried there had been a medical emergency."

Erwin's mind attempted to catch up with everything Adeline had told him. Apparently doctor/patient confidentiality was something he'd need to speak with Patty about. Even if she hadn't mentioned exactly why he'd been visiting the clinic, he didn't think it was the town's business that he'd visited her at all.

But then he landed on the fact that Adeline was under the impression that she'd tricked Jessie into going on a date with him.

"I appreciate your concern," he said. "But I think you're mistaken. It's true that I've visited Patty often as of late, and it may have led to some rash decisions. But I asked Jessie out on a date, and she chose to come—she wasn't tricked into it. No undue stress on my part."

That was a bit of a fabrication. There had been nothing but undue stress recently. But he didn't want Jessie knowing that he was freaking out about what was happening between them, and if he bared his soul to Adeline, it wouldn't be ten minutes before Jessie knew as well.

"Oh, good. Thank you for clearing that up for me," Adeline said. Even though her words were slow, it seemed her mind was racing, trying to put everything together. And Erwin couldn't help but wonder what it was that she wasn't saying.

It was another moment before Adeline's thoughtful expression cleared, and she said, "Glad to see that all is well." She gave a little wave, then turned and sprinted back the way she had come.

Erwin had an uneasy feeling as he watched her figure shrink in the distance that he'd revealed more than Adeline had originally been aware of.

He might need to warn Jessie about that.

Erwin never did get the chance to tell Jessie about his and Adeline's encounter. As soon as he returned to the restaurant, he needed to deal with a plumbing issue in the kitchen. He was just wiping the sweat and dirt from his face when Jessie burst in, unannounced.

"What possessed you to do a thing like that?" she demanded. "You're always going on about not trusting Adeline with secrets because of her tricks and pranks. It's not true, of course, she's a good friend, but everyone has their limits, and you went and told her the single most important thing not to tell anyone. Ever."

It seemed Jessie had found out on her own. Most likely from Adeline herself.

"I thought she already knew," Erwin protested. "She was asking if I was okay, saying she'd tried calling. It seemed she was feeling guilty. Adeline claimed she'd been the one to instigate things between us and that it was..." Erwin's words slowed. "That it was because of her that you'd met me for dinner. That she'd tricked you into it."

Realization settled over him.

He felt lightheaded.

Erwin had known that just because he and Jessie had kissed, that didn't mean they were getting back together, or the past thirty years had been forgotten. But he'd at least thought that everything leading up to it had been real.

"Everything has been about these stupid challenges, hasn't it?" Erwin asked. He couldn't believe he'd been so stupid. "You showed up for our date because Addie told you to. Is that why you kissed me, as well? Because you wanted to win a chocolate recipe?"

"Of course not," Jessie said, looking offended that he'd think such a thing. She couldn't blame him, though, when everything pointed to that conclusion. "Yes, there have been challenges. But the only one directly related to you instructed me to talk to you without fighting. Not something we've been good at the last few decades, and frankly, it was nice. Talking to you without wanting to kill you by the end of the conversation."

It was Erwin's turn to be offended. "That seems a bit dramatic, don't you think?" Then again, Jessie was the very definition of dramatic.

She released a long sigh. "The point is, Addie never instructed me to kiss you. She'd never cross that line. And neither would I. Not for a chocolate recipe. She'd asked me to say yes to everything for a day—the day you asked me out on the date. That's it. Everything else, well, that's been all me."

Pink tinged Jessie's cheeks, and she seemed embarrassed that she hadn't been strong-armed into everything that had happened between them.

"You're embarrassed that you chose to kiss me," Erwin said.

Jessie hesitated. "I don't think embarrassed is the right word. Confused, yes. And if word travels through town before I figure out how I feel about—this," she gestured between the two of them, "then, yes, I do think I'll be embarrassed."

Jessie likely wouldn't have gone to dinner—wouldn't have given Erwin a chance if not for Adeline. He should thank her, he supposed. Unless Adeline spread the gossip about their kiss. Then he'd hold it against her for the rest of her life—never allowing her to forget. The last thing he wanted was for Jessie to be embarrassed.

He could only imagine the fallout that would result from something like that.

"Hold on a moment," Erwin said, lifting a finger. "It just occurred to me that you did say no to me that evening. When I proposed."

Jessie gave a slow nod. "Yes, and I told Adeline that I'd failed the challenge."

"And yet..."

"She gave me a second chance." And then Jessie tossed

a greeting card onto the counter beside Erwin. "Your challenge for the day."

She spun around and left as quickly as she had come, not allowing him to open the challenge in her presence.

Erwin held his breath as he slit the envelope open and pulled the card out. It held just two words.

Fix it.

If only it were that easy. He supposed the only sure way to ensure Adeline didn't tell anyone was a sudden case of isolated amnesia. He wondered how he would manage that.

Well, he needed to at least try, didn't he?

18

J essie went straight home from Erwin's, not trusting herself to go anywhere else. She knew it wasn't fair of her to expect Erwin to fix things with Adeline all on his own. Sure, it was his fault she knew about their kiss. But in his defense, many people had accidentally revealed secrets to Adeline over the years without ever realizing it. Adeline was good at that.

When Adeline had confronted Jessie about the kiss, Jessie had been so shocked, she hadn't been able to lie. No words had come, and the truth must have been written all over her face.

Jessie Carter had kissed her ex-fiancé, Erwin.

And she'd liked it.

She desperately hoped Adeline hadn't picked up on that last part.

Maybe it wouldn't be such a bad thing if people knew.

It would force Jessie and Erwin to finally confront this thing head on.

But what if it wasn't what Jessie wanted? Or what Erwin wanted?

Then things would get worse. So much worse.

If that happened, Jessie really would have to consider moving from her hometown. Because there was no way she would be able to face her friends and neighbors after that.

Adeline had sworn she wasn't going to tell anyone about the recent development, and Jessie desperately wanted to believe her. Adeline was the kind of person who would drop everything to help her friends, and she would never purposely hurt those around her. Especially Jessie.

But the kind of gossip that Adeline was sitting on...this was huge. If the roles were reversed, Jessie was unsure what she would do. She certainly wouldn't intend on telling people. But that also didn't mean she would be successful.

Jessie paced the living room. Had Erwin gone over to talk to Adeline yet? What would he say? Maybe Jessie had made a mistake. She didn't trust Erwin to not make things worse.

Her gaze landed on the plaid envelope on the counter. Her own challenge for the day. She hadn't dared open it yet. What had started as an exciting addition to her life had quickly turned to dread.

Only ten days left, she reminded herself.

Jessie forced herself to close the distance and pick the card up. She wasn't going to let Adeline win. Not like this.

Relief flooded through her as she slid the card out of the envelope and read it.

Go to the movie theater.

Sneak in popcorn, candy, and a drink.

Watch Raiders of the Lost Ark.

The old movie theater in town didn't play movies most days during the off-season. Usually only a couple of times a month, if that. There wasn't even a regular schedule. You just had to check the announcement board on the front of the theater, and hopefully they were playing one that week. Or you'd discover that you had unfortunately missed it by a day, which was usually the case.

And you never knew which movie would be playing.

Jessie hadn't been to a movie in years—had she told Adeline about that? And it had been even longer since she'd snuck food into the theater. She'd make sure to tip whoever happened to be working that evening to ease her conscience.

She slipped the card back into its envelope.

Raiders of the Lost Ark. Jessie couldn't remember when she'd last seen that one, or whom she had last watched it with. Erwin, probably.

He loved those kinds of movies, and Indiana Jones had always been a favorite.

Jessie couldn't help but wonder if Erwin would also be attending the movie, or if he even knew about it.

She'd feel guilty if she didn't at least let him know it was playing. It would eat at her the entire time she was at the theater and steal any joy she would have had while watching it.

Jessie picked up the phone and dialed the restaurant. He probably wasn't even there, and she would need to leave a message. She had instructed him to fix things with Adeline, after all, and that would take time.

"Hello." Erwin's voice caught Jessie off guard when he answered after the first ring.

"Oh. Hi, Erwin," Jessie said, her thoughts stumbling over themselves.

A pause.

"Jessie? You okay?" Concern laced his words.

She tried to ignore what that did to her. "Yeah. Of course. Just surprised you answered is all. Thought I'd be leaving a message."

Another pause.

"You called when you thought I wouldn't be home. Because you wanted to relay a message without having to actually talk to me." He was using his matter-of-fact tone, and Jessie couldn't tell what he was thinking. "Do you want me to hang up and you can call again?"

Jessie stifled a laugh. He'd done a good job of masking his emotions, but the humor was still there. He was teasing her. She released an exaggerated sigh. "I suppose you'll do." She laughed again but then added, "It's not that I didn't want to talk to you. I just assumed you'd be out stalking Adeline at her shop."

"Oh, no, I already took care of that."

Jessie was quiet while her brain attempted to catch up. "You managed to fix things with Adeline in the last forty-five minutes?"

"Yup. Anything else you needed, or were you just calling to check up on me?" Normally Erwin would have said something like that with frustration or annoyance. Not this time, though. He seemed amused.

Jessie finally found her voice. "No. Something else. I saw that Indiana Jones is playing at the theater tonight. Thought you might want to know."

This time it was Erwin who didn't speak. He'd been quiet so long, Jessie wondered if he'd hung up.

"You still there?" she asked.

A cough on the other end. "Um...yeah. Indiana Jones, huh? The new one?"

"Oh gosh, no. I would never have made a phone call for that. The original. *Raiders of the Lost Ark*."

An indistinguishable sound from the other end. "Why are you telling me this?" he finally asked.

"Because I know you enjoy Indiana Jones and thought you might want to see it. Who knows what movie the theater will play next? Probably something like the fourteenth *The Land Before Time*. They never knew when to stop with that series."

"Jess, *Raiders of the Lost Ark* was the last movie we saw in the theater together. Before...you know."

How did Jessie not remember that? Maybe she'd been suppressing it because of what had occurred after. But still...that was a big thing to completely block out.

"And now it's back," she said. "Maybe it's a sign. Or not. But what do you say? Would you like to see a movie with me tonight?"

Jessie hadn't planned to ask Erwin to accompany her, but the challenge didn't say she had to go alone. And it was something they both enjoyed. It would be silly to sit in separate rows.

And she could admit that she was in recovery mode—she didn't want him to know she'd completely forgotten the significance of the movie. So, here she was, pretending that she knew, and that she didn't care. Hadn't fazed her one bit.

She crossed her arms to keep her hands from shaking as she awaited Erwin's answer.

"All right. But I need to know upfront what this is. Are we paying for ourselves, or is this you asking me out on a date? Because I don't feel comfortable with you being the one to take charge. Call me old-fashioned, but there is a way these things are done."

Oh. Jessie hadn't thought she'd need to place a label on...whatever this was. But it was about time she didn't overthink things and let the pieces fall where they may.

"It's a date, and I'm the one asking, so get used to it,

Erwin. Times have changed over the past thirty years. You can pay for my ticket, but I'm supplying the snacks. If you would like to open doors for me, that is acceptable. You can choose if you'd like to pick me up at my house, but it makes logical sense if I pick you up from the restaurant since it's on the way."

Wow. That felt good.

Stunned silence filled the phone line.

"All right. I can live with that," Erwin said. "But others will be at the movie. It will probably be packed. Everyone in town will see us."

"Are you embarrassed to be seen with me, Erwin?" Jessie asked.

"Of course not, but—"

"I've cared for far too long what the town says about me, and that ends today. We're going on a date tonight, Erwin. And we're going to have fun. See you at six o'clock."

Jessie then hung up, her energy spent. She'd need a nap to recover from that.

But it had been worth it.

Tonight, Jessie was going out on the town.

19

Erwin hadn't seen Jessie fired up like that in a long time—at least in a way that wasn't directed at him. And he liked it. The kind of passion Jessie had for life, he'd never had it to the same degree. And when she'd no longer been a part of his life, he had felt the immense loss of that energetic excitement for life.

Now, he didn't know what to do with it.

Anxiety pulled at Erwin, and he attempted to shove it back. Technically he and Jessie had already been out to dinner. That counted as a date. Even if it had been a disastrous one. And it had felt more like a business meeting than a romantic rendezvous.

Erwin moved to his closet and frowned. There weren't many options to choose from. He supposed she had seen it all dozens of times, so whatever he wore, there would be no surprises.

After a moment of deliberation, he determined that changing clothes would need to wait. If Erwin was going to make it through the movie without falling asleep, he would need to take a power nap, and he wasn't about to wrinkle his date clothes before even making it out the front door.

ONE POWER NAP, early dinner, and a change of clothes later, Erwin waited nervously by the front door. He should have bought Jessie a bouquet of flowers. Or at the very least something that showed he was serious about making up for lost time.

You don't know that's what she wants. There's too much anger and resentment to just go back to how things were.

That was true. And yet...something had shifted. He didn't know how, or when. Maybe it was the cup of hot chocolate on that cold day a few weeks earlier. But for the first time in decades, Erwin felt he might have a chance at happiness.

And he wasn't going to lose that.

Erwin grabbed a pair of scissors and walked outside, hoping to find at least one flower still in bloom. His gaze scanned the landscape, finally landing on a rose that had somehow withstood the test of the elements, almost like it was waiting for him.

He took a step toward it but paused when Jessie appeared in front of the restaurant at the same moment.

Would it be awkward if he gave her the flower, even as he cut it?

She lifted her hand in greeting, her eyes lighting up when she saw him. A large purse hung over one shoulder and she shifted it, as if it was heavy.

Jessie had never looked lovelier. Even when they'd been young, she hadn't matched the grace she had now. She wore a denim jacket over a long flowered dress, her toes peeking out at the bottom. She tucked a strand of hair behind one ear, her gaze dropping, as if she was embarrassed.

Maybe Erwin had been staring. He did that sometimes without realizing it.

"I was about to cut a flower for you," he said. "I'm sorry, I didn't think of going to Natalie's shop earlier."

Jessie hurried over, the large purse whacking her in the side as she placed a hand on his, preventing him from moving forward with the plan. "Don't you dare cut that poor thing. It's the only one who managed to survive this long, and you want to give it an early death."

Erwin laughed. They may have grown older, but Jessie would always be the same strong-willed woman he'd fallen in love with. And as much as that strong will had tormented him over the previous years, he suddenly found it endearing.

"All right. I'm sorry. Let me just put these scissors back inside, and we can go."

Jessie removed her hand from his, and he retreated to the restaurant, trying to ignore the tingles that Jessie's touch had left behind.

Not even a minute later, the two of them were walking down the road and toward the theater. It was quiet between them, neither one seeming to know what to say. With Jessie, that was a rare feat, but it had been increasingly common as of late.

Ever since Adeline's challenges.

Which brought up a question Erwin needed answered before they arrived at the theater.

"When I talked with Addie earlier..." Erwin said, his words slow. He needed to phrase this just right. "I was assured that she wouldn't be meddling in our affairs, and that she had no interest in spreading rumors. She even agreed to the stipulation that if she told anyone about... you know what..."

"Us kissing," Jessie said, filling in the blank that Erwin had purposely kept vague. He didn't want to think about it, let alone talk about it. That would only get his hopes up.

He cleared his throat. "Yes. Anyway, if she tells anyone, she has to give you her entire recipe book. Or a copy of it, at any rate."

Jessie raised an eyebrow and nodded, looking impressed. Warmth spread into Erwin's cheeks, and he forced himself to continue.

"But I have to ask. This date. The movie. Is this just

another one of her challenges? Are we here because you have something to prove?"

Jessie hesitated. Never a good sign.

"She did challenge me to go to the movie tonight," she said. "It's been ages since I've gone to one. They end so late, you know. But there was nothing in the challenge about inviting you. Nothing about a date."

Erwin had his doubts. This still had Adeline written all over it.

"She must have known this movie held special significance for us," Erwin pressed on. "Must have known I liked it. She knew you would invite me."

Jessie released an exasperated sigh. "Does it matter if she thought I might invite you? The point is that it was my choice. And maybe she thought there might have been a chance. But it wasn't one that she was in control of. I wanted to be here with you, Ernie."

The way Jessie was looking at him—it was genuine. She was telling the truth. It sent warmth through his chest. "I'm sorry. You're right," he said. "After everything we've been through, not even Adeline could get you here if you didn't want to be."

Jessie gave a satisfied nod. "Darn right." Then she surprised him by taking his hand as they continued toward the theater.

Erwin was tempted to pull his hand from hers, but he'd missed this so much. Jessie's hands may have aged over the years, but they were still as soft as he remembered, and they still fit his perfectly.

"You're not afraid of people seeing?" he asked as the theater came into view. All of his hard work to make sure Adeline didn't spread rumors would be in vain if anyone saw the two of them walking hand in hand. And he could only imagine the uproar that would follow.

"I was," she admitted. "Before showing up at your house tonight. Wondered if it was a mistake, asking you to the movies." She paused, like she was collecting her thoughts. "I wanted to invite you, so I did. That's all there is to it. I'm done worrying about what others will say. From here on out, I'm doing what makes me happy."

Erwin tried to suppress a laugh, and it came out as a snort instead.

She shot him a small smile. "I know I'm one to talk, considering that I'm usually the one interfering with everyone else's lives. But I only do it because I care about them."

Erwin raised an eyebrow.

"And because it feels good to know something that no one else does," she added. "But mostly because I care."

Even though Erwin liked to give Jessie a hard time, he knew she loved everyone in town as if they were family. She'd always been like that.

He'd always been a little jealous that she'd had this unconditional love that seemed to elude him. Erwin loved the town too, but not in the same way as Jessie. No one could love in the same way she did.

"I like that," he said. "We could all do with a little more happiness." He paused. "So, being here with me tonight. That makes you happy?"

As soon as he asked it, he wished he could take it back. He didn't want to know the answer. Didn't want to hear her say that she'd merely been bored. Or lonely. And being here with him was better than not being with anyone at all.

Because Erwin hadn't been able to make Jessie happy for a very long time. In fact, he usually made things worse.

But she gave him a thoughtful smile, her eyebrows knitted in concentration as she considered the question. "Yes," she finally said. "I never thought I'd see the day, but being here with you—it makes me happy. Maybe we just had to stop fighting long enough for me to see it."

It was true that arguments and competition had been the basis of their relationship since their breakup all those years ago. They'd never given each other the chance to be anything other than that.

"I'm happy with you too," he said, giving her hand a squeeze.

There. The words were out there. He couldn't take them back. And he didn't want to.

Until they entered the theater lobby and he realized most of the town was there. It didn't take long for them to be spotted. For the side glances and whispers to start.

Not everyone tried to be discreet.

"Lord almighty, no wonder you've been under a lot of stress," Patty half-yelled across the lobby. "How long have you two been sitting on this secret?"

And so it began.

20

Jessie had known there would be talk. That people would notice. But she had taken Erwin's hand because she didn't want the town to find out about them from anyone else. She wanted to see where things could go with Erwin, and she didn't want to sneak around to do it.

She'd seen how hiding a relationship had affected other couples over the years—how it had nearly done them in—and she didn't want that for herself.

Erwin had been right. Their clocks were ticking and there was no time to waste.

Except, Jessie wasn't afraid of dying. She was afraid of not living.

And after the kiss the previous evening, she'd realized she'd been missing out on so much. Maybe this thing with Erwin was doomed. It most likely was. But no one would be able to say she hadn't given it a fighting chance.

Patty rushed over to them, never afraid to speak her mind. "Seriously, how did we not know about this?" She nodded to Jessie and Erwin's entwined hands.

Jessie could tell he was tempted to pull away, his grip loosening. She didn't give him that chance. Her resolve, and her grip, strengthened.

"Because I don't tell you everything, Patty. This was on a need-to-know basis," Jessie said.

Patty raised an eyebrow and turned her gaze on Erwin.

"Need-to-know," he repeated.

"But you two can't be in the same room without arguing. Are you telling me that's all been a show?" she asked, still incredulous.

Unfortunately, no, it hadn't been. But before Jessie could formulate a response, Erwin straightened, and his gaze steadied on Patty.

"I've been putting on a show my entire life. Until now," he said. "Now if you'll excuse me, I need to purchase tickets for Jessie and me." Then he leaned over, kissed Jessie on the cheek, and walked to the ticket booth.

Jessie had never been more attracted to Erwin than at that moment. She could still feel where his lips had pressed against her cheek, and she was so distracted by it that she didn't even realize Patty had continued to speak to her.

"Oh, wow, you have it bad," Patty said, and Jessie finally

managed to turn her attention away from where Erwin was slipping his wallet into his back pocket.

Jessie managed a laugh. "What are you talking about?"

"Girl, you can't tear your eyes away from him. In fact, the look you have right now—it reminds me a lot of when you two were dating all those years ago." When Jessie gave Patty a dubious look, she said, "Don't think I don't remember."

Heat rushed into Jessie's cheeks, and she smoothed down her hair as Erwin rejoined them. "Good to see you, like always," she said to Patty as they moved away from her and towards the auditorium.

Erwin stopped and handed the usher, Craig, their tickets. Really, they were just raffle tickets, and Craig was just checking to make sure they had paid. There were no assigned seats.

"I thought you were buying the snacks," Erwin said, noting Jessie's empty arms. "Not that I'm complaining. I'd be happy to go buy us some popcorn. You were just so emphatic earlier that you would be the one to take care of it."

Jessie raised a finger to her lips, hoping he understood to not press the subject. "Let me consider it for a moment while we find our seats."

His eyebrows quirked, and she wasn't certain he'd understood the message, but Craig motioned them through, and Jessie followed Erwin to the fifth row from the front.

"Awfully close, isn't it?" Jessie said. "I know our eyesight isn't what it used to be. But neither is my neck."

Erwin looked like he was going to argue with her, but he stopped himself. "You might have a point."

As Jessie followed him back two rows, she wondered if she liked this new relationship with Erwin. Even when they'd been dating, there had been banter between the two. Disagreements and compromise. But it had been fun and made things interesting. Not at the end of things, of course, but before then.

Now, it seemed Erwin was afraid to disagree on anything, or at the very least, make his opinion known.

Jessie didn't like this new dynamic.

"Why did you want the seats up there?" Jessie asked, nodding toward the front of the theater.

Erwin hesitated, as if afraid she'd be annoyed.

"I want to know," she insisted.

"Because those seats have always been a little bit looser," he said. "They lean back a bit more than the others in the theater, and I can treat them similar to my recliner at home. Not too much, mind, or you end up in the lap of the person behind you. But they are quite comfortable."

Jessie watched as a family took the seats she and Erwin had just vacated. "Well, why didn't you say anything? We could have stayed. I wouldn't have minded."

"Because..." Erwin ran a hand through his hair and blew out a frustrated breath. "Because I don't know what to make of us, Jess. We're one argument away from landing back where we were. And maybe that's where we've always belonged. But if there is a chance in the world that we could make this work, this is it. And I don't want to blow it."

"The only way this is going to work is if you speak your mind," Jessie said. "I don't want you to agree with me about everything. I don't want to be afraid of having a difference of opinion. Because like it or not, Erwin, I'm still in love with you. And maybe this is a terrible idea—trying to start things back up again. But we can learn from our mistakes. We can make a second go of things and do it right this time. If you want to, of course. No pressure."

No pressure. Right. After she'd just declared her love for him in a crowded theater, in front of everyone.

Too late now, because Adeline had unleashed something in Jessie. A recklessness. An insatiable desire to have everything she'd missed out on. A need to be young again.

"Well, it just so happens that I love you too," Erwin said matter-of-factly. "But I'll love you even more if you tell me when I'm going to be getting my popcorn. I refuse to watch Indiana Jones without it."

"You think I'm hauling this giant purse around for fun?" Jessie grinned as she pulled it open, revealing a plastic bag filled with homemade popcorn, several smaller bags of candy, and two bottles of soda. "I have you covered."

Erwin's lips parted in surprise, his gaze darting around the auditorium, like he was nervous someone might have seen. Which was a distinct possibility, because from the moment they'd entered, they'd captured the attention of most of the attendees. "That's against the rules," he said, lowering his voice. "As a member of town council, you know that we don't make any profit from this theater. The only reason we show movies is to help cover the maintenance of the building so it doesn't have to be torn down. Everything we make goes toward it."

Guilt settled over Jessie, but right now she didn't want to think about rules and regulations. She just wanted to have fun. And yes, win the challenge. "I know, Erwin. And I'm generously donating to the building fund to make up for it. But don't you ever get tired of the rules?"

Erwin folded his arms and settled back in his seat. "You're feeling rebellious."

"Yes, I am."

He threw her a side glance. "That's Adeline's doing. You know better than anyone that we don't have rules for the sake of having rules. There's a purpose behind them."

"That's true. But I also know that many of Starlight Ridge's rules are for the sake of tradition. Because they are comfortable."

"Traditions are important too."

Jessie leaned in close. "Then you'll remember that the last time we watched *Raiders of the Lost Ark*, we snuck in food. Just like this."

Erwin stilled, and his gaze swung back to the giant bag

of food. "I'd totally forgotten about that," he said, his voice soft.

Jessie hadn't remembered at first, either. But once Erwin had mentioned their last movie date, it had all come flooding back.

"Please, Ernie," she said. "Let's just enjoy the night. Forget the people we've become, and let's remember who we were."

Erwin held her gaze, then gave a slow nod. "I'd like that." And then he stuck his hand into the purse and pulled out a bag of peanut M&M's. "These are mine, though."

Good. Because Jessie had bought those specially for him.

They settled back into their seats, Erwin's hand inching over and resting on her leg as the movie started. No previews in this theater...just straight to the point.

Jessie placed her hand over his and squeezed.

She didn't know if this moment could last, or if things would return to business as usual.

Regardless, she intended to enjoy it as long as he allowed her to.

21

E rwin and Jessie stayed in their seats as everyone else filed out, the end credits rolling in front of them.

"That was even better than I remembered," he said, leaning back with a satisfied smile. And the popcorn had been better than anything they could have purchased at the concession stand. He wouldn't admit that part, though, because it couldn't happen again.

Probably.

Or he could donate extra to the building fund at the next town meeting.

"I agree." Jessie smiled and stood, extending a hand toward Erwin. "And neither of us fell asleep, so that's always a plus." He took her hand, grunting as he stood. He'd forgotten what those seats did to his lower back.

"We didn't used to fall asleep," Erwin said, winking,

and then immediately hating himself for it. He wasn't the type to flirt. Not at his age.

A blush crept up Jessie's neck, and she glanced away. Okay, maybe the wink hadn't been so bad.

With Jessie's large purse now empty, she folded it, and Erwin carried out their trash.

"I know it's late," she said, linking her hand through his arm, "but I'm not quite tired yet. Would you enjoy a beach-side walk?"

Erwin hesitated. He'd love that, but things between Jessie and him—they were going too fast. He knew he was one to talk, considering he had proposed to her over the first dinner they'd shared in thirty years. But he was falling for her all over again. Seeing glimpses of the Jessie he'd once loved.

Truth be told, he'd never stopped loving Jessie. There had just been roadblocks preventing them from being together, and he hadn't bothered to try to knock them down. In fact, he'd built them higher, protecting himself from ever going through that kind of heartache again.

"We don't have to," she said quickly when he hadn't responded. "A silly thought." She removed her hand from his arm.

"It wasn't. And I would love that."

Erwin threw their trash in a can on their way out before taking Jessie's purse from her and tucking it under one arm.

"Quite the gentleman," she said, a teasing lilt to her voice.

"Always have been, even if you hadn't noticed." He winced. The words had come out harsher than he'd intended. That wasn't very gentlemanlike. And he could admit there had been many of those instances over the years. "Sorry. Old habits. And not good ones either."

Jessie released a sigh as she slipped her hand back through his arm. They were crossing the boardwalk, the shop windows darkened for the evening. It was peaceful. If Erwin could stay up late once in a while, he wouldn't mind getting used to this time of day.

"We've really made a mess of things, haven't we?" she said. "Sometimes I wonder if it's possible for us to dig our way out."

Erwin rested his free hand on hers. "Sure. If that's what we want."

They reached the edge of the beach and stopped for a moment. The moon and stars reflected off the ocean. It was moments like this when it seemed nothing could go wrong.

But Erwin knew all too well that the sun would eventually rise and illuminate all the flaws the darkness currently hid.

"I've wanted someone to share my life with for so long, I don't know what I'd do if it actually happened," Jessie finally said. "Stupid, huh? That I'm scared of the one thing I want."

Erwin chuckled. Not because it was funny but because it couldn't be truer. "I know exactly what you mean. And it's not stupid at all. Or if it is, then at least you have company."

Jessie started walking again, pulling Erwin after her. "It's nice. Being here. Talking with you. Almost like we're friends again."

Friends. Was that what Jessie thought of this as?

"It's not a bad thing, you know." He threw her a side glance. "To not want to be alone. But please don't pretend to enjoy my company. I don't want a pity companion. When I proposed to you...I thought it was out of regret. But I know better now."

Jessie didn't say anything right away, instead studying him. "You don't feel regret?"

From her downturned lips, Erwin realized she'd misunderstood him. "I do," he said quickly. "But that's not the reason I proposed to you—not the reason I want to spend time with you. I want to spend time with you because...you're you. No one makes me laugh the way you do. You don't know how difficult it has been over the years to pretend I didn't find you funny. Or how difficult it was not to rush to your home when I heard you were sick, just to see if you needed the company.

"That was why I proposed to you. Because more than the fear of dying alone was the fear of dying without you. I've avoided you for the past thirty years, because I didn't want you to see how much I missed you. How much I longed for us to reclaim what we'd had. Every time I do something even remotely enjoyable, I think, Jessie would have enjoyed this. And it breaks my heart every time. Knowing what we could have had—and what I threw away." He shook his head. "And people wonder why I'm so ornery. They would be too if they had to pass by the love of their life every day for thirty years and not be able to do anything about it."

"Oh, Erwin," Jessie said with a soft sigh. She stopped and pulled Erwin in, wrapping her arms around his neck.

He'd missed this. Jessie's touch. Her companionship. Her love.

"I should have sold my restaurant years ago," Erwin murmured into her hair. "Maybe then we'd have had a chance to grow old together."

Jessie pulled back, and Erwin immediately missed her touch. "It was more than you not walking away from the restaurant," she said. Her tone immediately put him on guard. "You acted like you didn't care. At least, about me. You care about everyone and everything in this town. And yet, you didn't show up to the grand opening of my bakery...or the final day when it closed. You go out of your way to shoot down every idea I propose at town meetings. You turned your back on me. I understand that our past was painful. But you never thought about how it affected *me*. How your actions might make *me* feel."

"I screwed up," he said, helpless. "I don't know what else there is to say. I don't believe I was the only one at fault for how things turned out—this disaster was a two-way street that both of us willingly went down. But I've told you that I regret it. And look how far we've come the last little while. We've overcome impossible odds, and we're finally moving on to forgiveness."

Jessie took Erwin's hands in hers, and relief flooded through him. "I do forgive you, Erwin. But I can't do this. Not again." She kissed him on the cheek and stepped back.

His head swam. What was happening here?

"But you held my hand. And said you love me. In front of everyone. I know you realize what a monumental thing that is. You must still have feelings for me, or you wouldn't have done that."

Jessie gave him a sad smile. "That's the problem, Ernie —I do love you. And that's why I need to walk away. I don't think I can survive another breakup like our first one. If we go any deeper—"

Her voice trailed off, and her gaze settled on the ocean, as if she couldn't bear to look at him any longer.

"If we call it quits now, there is no going back," he warned. "The fallout will be insurmountable. This will be our final goodbye."

She gave a little nod. "I know."

Those two little words were enough to crush Erwin's heart. His hope. His happiness.

But they also made his path very clear.

He needed to call back the lawyer he'd been avoiding.

Erwin had a restaurant to sell.

22

The next morning, Jessie stood outside Adeline's chocolate shop, gazing upwards at the lit sign. She didn't want to go in. Didn't want to talk about what had happened. But she had nowhere else to turn. Because as much as the town thought of Jessie as the mother of Starlight Ridge, she knew the truth. She was alone in the world.

That wasn't entirely true. Jessie had friends.

But she knew Caleb and Bree would be getting their toddler ready for the day, and Isaac and Leanne had their guests to take care of at the bed and breakfast.

Everyone else had their own lives.

Including Adeline.

But Jessie also knew that Adeline would drop everything at a moment's notice to help Jessie. That was why she had agreed to Addie's challenge. Jessie trusted her.

Unlike Erwin. What would happen if they had another argument—and they would. Should Jessie expect him to run away and avoid her the way he had the last time?

The front door to the shop opened, and Adeline squinted against the dark. "Jessie, is that you?"

Jessie didn't answer right away. Maybe she could sneak off and avoid this difficult conversation. Adeline would think it had been a cat. Or—

"It *is* you. What are you doing, staring at my store all creepy-like?" Adeline said, opening her door wider. "Get in here."

There went Plan A. There hadn't been a Plan B, so she followed Adeline into the store.

Jessie had done the right thing with Erwin. Hadn't she?

Perhaps she'd been too harsh. He did care about her. Like when he'd insisted she warm up with hot chocolate after her frolic through the ice-cold ocean.

But all those things Erwin had said about avoiding her —that wasn't the kind of man she needed. Someone who avoided conflict rather than work things out.

Adeline turned on a couple of lights. "I'd offer you a sample, but I just sealed my last box."

"It's okay. I don't need any truffles today."

Adeline gave Jessie a long look. "Everything okay?" She settled herself behind the counter. "If this is about today's challenge, I know it's a bit of an easy one, but it's because I felt like you needed a break after last night."

Challenge? For the first time since they'd started, Jessie

hadn't opened the envelope. She'd been too exhausted from a restless night's sleep. She didn't even remember where she'd placed it. On the counter, perhaps?

Jessie waved a hand. "No, haven't even had the chance to look at it."

"So, you're here before daylight because of Erwin." Adeline's eyebrows knit in concern.

Jessie nodded. This felt like deja vu from two weeks earlier. Two weeks. That meant Jessie would receive a box of chocolates the following day. Good thing that day's challenge would be easy. She didn't think she'd be able to manage anything more than that.

"Yesterday, I felt so sure of things," she told Adeline. "I'm the one who gives advice. I help others find their happily-ever-after. I should be better at this."

Adeline gave her an amused smile. "Everything is so clear, until your own emotions become involved."

Truer words had never been spoken.

"So, what do I do?" Jessie whispered. "I made a show out of us last night at the movie theater. Wanted everyone to know that Erwin and I—"

"That you were happy," Adeline finished for her.

Jessie nodded. "I've forgiven him for everything that happened in the past. But last night after the movie, when it was just him and me—no distractions—the memories flooded over me. I felt like I was drowning. I've forgiven, but I can't forget. He wants to pretend everything can go back to how it was. But we're both in different places now."

She paused. "No, I'm in a different place. Erwin still has his restaurant. And Donna. And what happens when we disagree on something? At the theater last night, he wouldn't voice his opinion on where we sat because he was afraid of an argument. We can't walk on eggshells for the rest of our lives, afraid of losing each other again. Might as well cut it off now, when it won't hurt as bad."

Adeline unsealed a box of truffles that sat behind the counter. "We're going to need this." She lifted the lid, offered a truffle to Jessie, then popped one in her own mouth and chewed slowly, giving herself more time to think. "You keep blaming Erwin. Saying it's he who's avoiding the hard stuff. That you can't forget everything he's done. But he's trying. Hard. And you're cutting things off just in case it doesn't work out in the future. From where I'm sitting, you both have your issues. But if it doesn't work out, it's not going to be Erwin's fault. It will be both of yours. Just like it was both of you at fault thirty years ago. So start taking responsibility for your contributions, or you're right, it's not going to work."

Jessie stared. She was used to Adeline's blunt nature, but it had never been directed at her in this way.

And Adeline didn't look at all sorry for it.

Because she was right. Jessie hadn't avoided Erwin since the breakup, because she'd felt no shame. None of what had transpired had been her fault. It had been all Erwin.

Or so she'd thought.

"It might be too late," Jessie said.

Adeline lifted a shoulder. "Maybe. But you'll never know unless you try."

Okay. Jessie would try.

And she'd apologize.

Because that was what mature adults did.

A pit formed in her stomach.

She wasn't certain she qualified as a mature adult.

And she wasn't certain she could do this.

JESSIE PACED the living room with her phone to her ear, the ringing driving her to the brink of madness. Did Erwin know it was her calling? Was that why he wasn't answering?

"Hello?"

The sound of Erwin's voice made Jessie lose her own momentarily. She was suddenly unsure what to say. Forgot why she'd called. Almost like the first time they'd spoken on the phone as teenagers.

She managed to regain her train of thought and blurted out, "Thanksgiving."

Real smooth, Jess.

Jessie sucked in a long breath. "We need to start putting together Thanksgiving dinner, or the town won't have one to attend in two weeks. You can decide all the details, and I'll act as support."

A voice in the background. Erwin wasn't alone.

"Now's not a great time, Jessie. Can we do this later?"

Jessie had thought he'd be thrilled she was no longer fighting him on this—that she'd given him complete control.

Someone spoke again. A man's voice.

"You working the restaurant today?" she asked.

"No, no. Nothing like that."

This time the man's voice in the background was louder. More urgent. "Erwin, I have another appointment after this. You said you wanted to sign. But this is the last time I'm coming out here. Your last chance to sell. My client won't be toyed with like this."

Sale.

"Erwin, you're not selling Seaside Bay, are you?" Jessie didn't know why that thought made her panic. Seaside Bay was half the reason that she and Erwin had broken up all those years ago. But the thought of Erwin no longer having the restaurant, it didn't sit right with her. That was his pride and joy.

"I'm sorry, Jessie, I really do have to go."

And then the man had the audacity to hang up on her.

But Jessie knew what she'd heard. Erwin was selling Seaside Bay.

Not if she had anything to say about it.

It was times like these that Jessie wished she owned a car. She threw on a coat and grabbed her bicycle from the garage. She didn't know the last time she'd ridden it, preferring to walk everywhere she went. But desperate times called for desperate measures.

She had to stop Erwin from doing something he'd regret.

Aside from his dogs, Seaside Bay had been Erwin's baby that he'd nurtured and cared for all these years. Yes, maybe it had been the cause of the end of their relationship. But Erwin wasn't in his right mind. This late-life crisis was messing with him—making him do things he normally wouldn't.

Like propose marriage.

She wasn't about to let selling Seaside Bay be added to the list of stupid things he'd done.

And so Jessie wobbled away on a bike whose tires weren't completely filled, but it would get her where she needed to be.

Probably.

Because Jessie needed to stop that lawyer.

23

Erwin had finally returned the lawyer's calls after receiving a voicemail telling Erwin that if he didn't respond, the lawyer's client wouldn't be trying again.

This was his last chance.

Erwin didn't like feeling forced into a situation he wasn't prepared for. But he had to make a choice, or the choice would be made for him.

Now that the lawyer was there, though, in his apartment, Erwin was second-guessing his decision.

"You're stalling," the lawyer said, pushing the papers in front of him on the kitchen table. "You've had ample time to read through the documents, and you said you were ready to move forward. If I walk through that door, per my client's instructions, I'm not allowed to return. This is it."

Yes, yes, Erwin understood that.

And after Jessie's declarations the previous evening,

he'd come to the conclusion that he was ready to make the move.

Seaside Bay was holding him back. Erwin had poured his whole life into the place, only to find thirty years later that he had been left empty-handed. Still alone. Nothing to show for his life but a seafood restaurant. Admittedly it had the best shrimp anyone had ever tasted.

But still, he'd done nothing more than feed people.

Donna came running into the kitchen, a ball in her mouth. She wanted to play fetch.

"Not now, Donna. When I'm finished here, okay?"

Donna pushed her muzzle onto Erwin's lap and dropped the ball. He chuckled, but the smile faded when the lawyer gave him a pointed look.

"Later," he whispered to Donna, dropping the ball onto the floor.

The golden retriever looked disappointed, and she lay at his feet, her head resting on her paws.

"It's not like that," he said. "I just have a few papers to sign first, that's—"

A frantic knocking on the back door to the restaurant interrupted his thought. It was the entrance he used to access the apartment. Now the doorbell.

The lawyer groaned. "Are you kidding me?"

Erwin hesitated, his gaze jumping to his apartment door, to the murderous-looking lawyer, and back to the door. He held up a finger. "Just one minute." The knocking grew louder.

He stood and moved to the window. Shifting the curtains a fraction, he peeked out.

Jessie.

Maybe he could pretend he wasn't home.

"I see you, Erwin," she called.

Or not.

He opened the window. "Now's not a good time for a planning session," he called down. "Give me an hour."

Jessie didn't seem interested in waiting. Instead, she opened the back door and thundered up the staircase. The apartment doorknob twisted, and before Erwin had time to react, Jessie was standing in his entryway. He was pretty sure that counted as breaking and entering. Or at least entering. And he moved to block her way.

"Jessie, please. Come back later. I don't have time for this right now."

Jessie moved toward him so quickly, he had to take a step back, nearly tumbling as he did. "Why, so you can sell Seaside Bay? No. I won't let you."

Erwin stared. His mind had gone blank, and all he could manage to do was blink. "How do you know about that?"

"I heard your *friend* in the background of our phone call. But you'll regret it, Ernie. You will. This place was your dream. And you've done amazing things with it."

Jessie's gaze... It was so intense. Genuine. Like she really did mean what she was saying.

But Jessie hated Seaside Bay. She'd never even eaten there—not once.

"Why are you here, Jess? You don't care about the restaurant." Erwin took a couple more steps backward. He wished she'd leave. She was making him doubt himself. And he didn't need that right now. Erwin needed to be able to let it go. Move on with the next phase of his life, whatever that might look like.

"No, but I do care about you. And Seaside Bay means everything to you. So what, you're getting older. Maybe your knees are crackling more than they used to and you have to wear reading glasses now. That's no reason to go selling off your dream. Any more reason than it was to propose to me."

That last statement.

Erwin wanted to think on it—analyze it. Ask what Jessie meant by it. But then the lawyer appeared in the kitchen doorway. "Erwin, I have ten minutes. Are we going to do this?"

Jessie didn't say anything this time. Merely watched him. But her eyes—they said everything she didn't need to. Pleading. Begging him to not make a mistake.

Would it be a mistake? He wasn't so sure. He'd have more money than he'd ever had in his life. Never having to worry about how many tourists they'd gotten that year. Able to finally enjoy life. Travel.

And the one thing that had stood between him and

Jessie for so many years would be removed from the equation.

"If there is even the possibility of us being together, I want to make sure there is nothing to stop us," he told Jessie. "Including the restaurant. I need to prove to you that you're more important than all of it."

Jessie shook her head. Her lips pulled up into a sad smile. "You don't need to prove anything, Ernie. I know you love me. That doesn't mean your restaurant isn't important, though. Keep it. I will support you. Whatever we do...we're going to do it together. How it was always meant to be. I'm sorry for the part I played in keeping us apart. But I won't be sabotaging our future any longer."

Erwin's head swam. He couldn't believe this was happening. What had made her change her mind?

The answer didn't matter.

Because Jessie was back.

"I can't sell the restaurant," he turned and told the lawyer.

The lawyer didn't seem the least bit surprised. "I know. Figured as much from the first time we met." He already had his briefcase packed up and in his hand, ready to go. With a final nod, he saw himself out.

"That makes one of us who knew what I'd do," Erwin said. "I've lost sleep for the past three weeks over this." His gaze landed on Jessie. "I just turned down the best price I'll ever get for Seaside Bay, by the way. Would have set us up for the rest of our lives."

"You could have taken it," Jessie said. She lifted a finger. "And don't you dare say I'm the reason you turned it down. You could have signed those papers weeks ago. And you could have signed them today."

Erwin loved how feisty Jessie could still get. He chuckled. "I wasn't going to blame you, but on second thought, I think I will."

Jessie frowned and folded her arms. "Excuse me? I stopped having any influence over your decisions a long time ago."

"I thought that was true, but it turns out I was wrong," Erwin said. "You've influenced every decision I've ever made. Because I've missed you, Jess. And when I realized all I have left is a lonely life that doesn't mean anything, I saw it for what it was. I screwed up. I chose Seaside Bay over you. And I thought that maybe, perhaps, if I sold it, there would no longer be anything in the way of us. If you chose not to give me a second chance, then at least I'd have plenty of money to drown my sorrows. Maybe move to the Caribbean, where I could spend my days with fancy drinks on the beach."

Jessie cocked an eyebrow. "You hate fancy drinks. And we have the best beach in the world right outside your restaurant here."

"Guess it's a good thing you decided to forgive me, then," he said with a wide smile. "Because you're right. I really do hate all those fancy drinks. They're weird. And pointless. Whatever happened to a good old-fashioned Orange Julius? Now, there's a drink I can get behind."

Jessie laughed but then dropped to one knee.

His breathing stalled. What was she doing? She better not be proposing. That was his job.

"Erwin Anderson, will you do me the honor of making you Orange Julius each morning for the rest of your life?"

Almost a proposal. But not quite.

He smiled and pulled her to her feet. "Is this your way of saying you changed your mind about my earlier proposal? Because I did propose first. You can't pretend I didn't."

Always the competition between those two.

"Fine. I'll admit you proposed first. If you let me be the first one to welcome the next newcomer to Starlight Ridge."

Erwin laughed and shook his head. "You've got yourself a deal."

He'd let her be first at everything if it meant they could be together while doing it.

Exactly how it was always meant to be.

24

Jessie placed her hands on her hips and looked up at the giant turkey that towered over her. Yes, Tommy was a bit worse for wear, but in her eyes, he was looking better than ever. Erwin had been right. They didn't need a new one.

Her gaze traveled over the beach. Tables had been placed on the sand, steadied by rocks. Bonfires dotted the landscape, providing both heat and light. It looked amazing. Sure, it was a little more inconvenient to carry the food down to the beach, but it was a new way to celebrate. And it fixed the problem of not having enough room.

The setup had been Jessie's idea. And Erwin had loved it. Surprisingly, the rest of the town had too. They wouldn't be able to use the karaoke machine because there was no power outlet, which meant there would be no opening speeches.

Judging by past years, it was probably better that way.

"This looks amazing," Adeline said, approaching Jessie after placing her pies on the serving table. "Seriously. We are going to have the best Thanksgiving ever. So glad we didn't do the rotating dinner. Whose idea was that, anyway?"

Erwin walked up behind Jessie and wrapped his arms around her waist. "Yours, I believe."

Adeline raised a skeptical eyebrow. "You sure? That seems like something Bree or Caleb would come up with."

"Definitely you," Jessie said, placing her hands on Erwin's. She tried to ignore the stares they were receiving from those in their vicinity. It was now common knowledge that she and Erwin were dating. But that didn't mean the shock had worn off. She hoped it would dissipate before too long.

"Huh. Well, good on you for overriding it. Because the bonfires combined with the tables full of food, close to the ocean—I mean, everything about it is perfect. And I'm glad you got rid of the iceless pitchers of water. Why did we have them every year? Nobody used those."

Erwin chuckled, his breath tickling Jessie's ear. "Do you want to say that you told me so?"

"You already did it for me," Jessie said with a laugh.

Someone called Adeline from the direction of the nearest bonfire. Her husband, Eli. "Hey, before I forget," she said, holding a folded piece of paper toward Jessie.

"My caramel truffle recipe. Don't let it fall into the wrong hands."

Jessie reverently took the paper. She'd just finished the last challenge that morning, and it felt weird to know she wouldn't have any more plaid envelopes showing up on her doorstep. The last month had been life-changing, and she was going to miss it.

"Thank you," Jessie said, slipping it into her purse. "I'll guard it with my life."

Adeline smiled. "I wouldn't expect anything less." And then she hurried over to where her husband awaited her. He was rubbing his arms, like he couldn't stay warm. As soon as Adeline reached him, Eli wrapped his arms around her, holding her close.

It was the kind of thing Jessie would have been quietly envious of a few months earlier.

Not anymore.

Except, Erwin's arms suddenly dropped from around her waist, and he stepped away. Jessie already missed his touch. "There is one more aspect of the Thanksgiving dinner that I may have forgotten to mention," he said. He held up one finger, as if to tell her to hold on a minute, and then he walked quickly to the side of the serving tables, where the town's jazz band was congregating.

Live music. Jessie liked the addition.

Isaac and Leanne walked up next to Jessie. Close behind them were Caleb and Bree, little Monty running circles around all of them.

"This is awesome," Isaac said. "You two should have gotten together years ago. Then maybe we wouldn't have had to suffer through all those lame Thanksgivings."

Leanne hit him on the arm with a look of warning. He raised a confused eyebrow, like he didn't understand what he'd said wrong.

"The timing had to be right," Bree said. "For Erwin and Jessie, and for new traditions."

Leanne nodded. "Exactly. And thankfully, it is time for both."

They all looked to Jessie for confirmation, but for once in her life, she had nothing to add. "Well said." She smiled as Caleb caught Monty and swung him up onto his shoulders, and then moved closer to the band.

Erwin picked up his saxophone. They didn't have any sound equipment down here, but Ewin did his best to be heard, shouting above the gathered crowd.

"I promised there would be no speeches this year, so forgive me for breaking my word. The boys and I are going to be playing throughout the Thanksgiving feast, and this first song means a lot to me. It's been years since I've played it, but for me, it was the catalyst to the rest of my life. Unfortunately, I lost my way, but God has given me a second chance. And none of it would have been possible without this song."

Erwin stepped back to stand with the rest of the jazz band, and they prepared to play.

Jessie didn't know what to expect, but the anticipation

made her hands sweat and her breaths shallow. She had already said yes to Erwin's proposal. They'd already decided they wanted to share the rest of their lives together, whatever that may look like. And Jessie had been keeping up her end by making Orange Julius every day. There was nothing more to prove.

But then the band began to play a song that Jessie hadn't heard for a long time—hadn't wanted to.

"Love Will Keep Us Together" by Captain and Tennille.

The tears that erupted from Jessie concerned her, and if Erwin's expression was anything to go by, they concerned him too.

But she couldn't hold them back. Because Erwin was right. This song had taken things to the next level for them. Had been the catalyst for everything good—and horrible—in their lives. And now they were starting over. Trying again.

And it was love that would keep them together. Just like the song promised.

The End

ALSO BY KAT BELLEMORE

BORROWING AMOR

Borrowing Amor

Borrowing Love

Borrowing a Fiancé

Borrowing a Billionaire

Borrowing Kisses

Borrowing Second Chances

STARLIGHT RIDGE

Diving into Love

Resisting Love

Starlight Love

Building on Love

Winning his Love

Returning to Love

ABOUT THE AUTHOR

Kat Bellemore is the author of the Borrowing Amor small town romance series. Deciding to have New Mexico as the setting for the series was an easy choice, considering its amazing sunsets, blue skies and tasty green chile. That, and she currently lives there with her husband and two cute kids. They hope to one day add a dog to the family, but for now, the native animals of the desert will have to do. Though, Kat wouldn't mind ridding the world of scorpions and centipedes. They're just mean.

You can visit Kat at www.kat-bellemore.com.

www.ingramcontent.com/pod-product-compliance
Lightning Source LLC
Chambersburg PA
CBHW020120180626
46812CB00006B/2669